HEART'S EASE

HEART'S EASE

Anne Stuart

This first world hardcover edition published 2010
in Great Britain and in the USA by
SEVERN HOUSE PUBLISHERS LTD of
9–15 High Street, Sutton, Surrey, England, SM1 1DF,
by arrangement with Harlequin Books.
First published 1984 in the USA in mass market format only.

British Library Cataloguing in Publication Data

Stuart, Anne (Anne Kristine)
  Heart's ease.
  1. Women scientists--Fiction. 2. Traffic accident
  victims--Virginia--Fiction. 3. Female friendship--
  Fiction. 4. Brothers and sisters--Fiction. 5. Love
  stories.
  I. Title
  813.5'4-dc22

 ISBN-13: 978-0-7278-6953-1   (cased)

All Severn House titles are printed on acid-free paper.

Severn House Publishers support The Forest Stewardship Council [FSC],
the leading international forest certification organisation. All our titles that
are printed on Greenpeace-approved FSC-certified paper carry the FSC logo.

Mixed Sources
Product group from well-managed
forests and other controlled sources
www.fsc.org Cert no. SA-COC-1565
© 1996 Forest Stewardship Council
FSC

Printed and bound in Great Britain by
MPG Books Ltd., Bodmin, Cornwall.

Chapter One

He was the sort of man she had always instinctively avoided. Such overpowering, almost ruthless good looks had the tendency to intimidate her. Combine that with a beautifully tailored three-piece suit and an almost aggressive air of self-assurance, and Cassie was glad she could be content to sit and observe him from a safe distance. It was almost as if she were watching someone in a movie—someone with unmistakable star quality and charisma.

He was quite tall, easily topping most of the people around him. His body was leanly muscled beneath the charcoal-gray suit, and he held himself with a faint arrogance that was nevertheless attractive. His hair was thick and black, curling slightly above his collar, his cheekbones high, his nose strong, his mouth drawn in a thin line that still couldn't disguise the sensuality that lurked there.

But his eyes were what captivated Cassie, the eyes that wandered around the moderately crowded regional air terminal and slid over Cassie without a trace of interest. Clearly the outstanding feature in his narrow tanned face, they were a luminous silver-blue set under high winged brows. The kind of eyes, Cassie thought dreamily, that would make a grown woman weep. And, truthfully, she was just as glad those extraordinary eyes had no interest in her whatsoever. Her life was complicated enough.

Reluctantly Cassie tore her gaze away from her paragon to search for Bran Rathburne. There were several possibilities, all the approximate age and type that Cassie had decided upon, but they were all moving through the terminal with a sense of purpose that suggested no interest whatsoever in an unknown Ms. O'Neill. Well, he'd simply have to find her. She turned her eyes back to the tall elegant figure that had fascinated her and watched with interest as he strode purposefully across to a stern-looking female in her late fifties. The conversation that ensued was brief and to the point, and he moved away, scanning the crowds once more with those silver-blue eyes.

Again they slid over Cassie, catching her glance for a brief, disinterested moment before moving on. Now a trace of pique combined with her relief. "Don't be absurd," she told herself in a small whisper. "He's nothing but trouble." Trouble was once again on the move, heading across the terminal to accost another female. This one was a few years younger, perhaps in her early fifties, with short-cropped gray hair, men's glasses, and a pugnacious expression. An equally brief conversation followed, and Trouble moved on, his beautiful mouth getting grimmer all the time, his silver-blue eyes wintry with anger. With dawning horrified realization Cassie watched him move once more toward another elderly lady, this one a few feet away from her.

"Ms. O'Neill?" he questioned the sixtyish matron. His voice sent an involuntary thrill down Cassie's backbone. She had heard it before, of course, over the telephone that morning. But now he was attempting a measure of courtesy, and the slightly husky timbre was as sexy as his long leanly muscled frame.

"I wish I were, my boy." The lady chuckled, shaking her head before moving away from him.

Slowly, reluctantly, with a burning feeling in the pit of her stomach, Cassie rose to her full height. The movement caught his attention, and for the third time that morning his eyes swept over her. This time his gaze held hers, and Cassie felt her pulse begin to race.

Throwing back her shoulders, she took a step toward him, fully aware of the incongruous impression she made. He would see a tall slender young woman, looking far younger than her twenty-eight years, the lean-fitting jeans and bulky sweater, the coronet of braids around her too-youthful face, contributing to the effect. And he was hardly likely to be bowled over by her beauty, she thought cynically. Her best feature, large golden-brown eyes, were currently hidden behind thin wire-rimmed glasses that she scarcely needed, and her lightly freckled uptilted nose and overgenerous mouth weren't likely to endear her to the scowling man. With her chestnut hair flowing free and a smile on her face, Cassie would be almost pretty, but at the moment she didn't feel in the least like smiling. "She may wish she were," Cassie managed in a calm drawl, "but for some reason I wish I weren't."

"Weren't what?" he said blankly, still staring at her, somewhat bemused.

"Cassandra O'Neill."

It would have been nice to see those silver-blue eyes lighten in self-deprecating humor, to see that sensuous mouth curve into a smile, but, of course, it was too much to hope for, and just as well. The man was too devastatingly attractive as he was, staring down at her with narrowed furious eyes and an unpleasantly mocking smile on his lips. "Do you enjoy playing people for fools, Ms. O'Neill?" There was the same cynical emphasis on her title, and Cassie's hackles rose.

"You took up the role quite readily," she replied, keeping her temper in check. "I had no idea you thought I was middle-aged until you hung up on me this morning. And you failed to arrange our meeting, so how was I to know that the man trying to pick up elderly ladies was Bran Rathburne and not some masher with peculiar tastes?"

It was not the best possible response, she realized belatedly. She should have tried to placate him. Rathburne simply continued to stare at her, contempt and something else she couldn't quite fathom in his eyes.

"Where are your bags?" he demanded abruptly after she felt sufficiently uncomfortable at the long silence.

Grabbing her duffel bag, determined not to surrender it to him, she replied, "Just this."

He made no effort to take it. "Good." Without another word he turned his tall, straight, undeniably beautiful back on her and strode out of the terminal, his long, long legs making quick work of the distance. Despite her above-average height, it was all Cassie could do to keep up with him, and the duffel bag, loaded as it was with books, along with her clothing, was heavier than she had expected. When she finally reached the parking lot, he was way ahead of her, standing by a long, sleek silver Jaguar that was the twin to his sister's presumably smashed black one. With studied rudeness he opened the door and climbed in, waiting impatiently behind the wheel while she fumbled with her duffel bag and the low-slung legroom. Without a word he put the high-powered monster in gear, and they were flying across the spring countryside at speeds that made Cassie, still not quite recovered from her turbulent plane ride, slightly green around the gills.

Leaning back against the butter-soft leather seat, Cassie shut her tired eyes. She only wished she could shut out her jumbled thoughts as easily. The hostility and contempt of the man beside her was a palpable thing, nudging at her when all she wanted to do was forget the tangled mess her life had become in the last two weeks. She had never expected that beautiful spring morning that had started out so well to lead to this series of catastrophes....

Cassie had stormed out of Dr. Thompson's office, quivering with all the rage and bewildered indignation an almost-twenty-eight-year-old of spotless principles and faultless conduct could muster. That they would dare...would dare...!

She marched through the hall, hands thrust into the pockets of the white coat that fluttered about her tall slim figure, all too aware of the shocked, disapproving, disbelieving glances of her fellow workers as she headed toward her small office. Unconsciously she squared her shoulders and raised her head, her usually warm brown eyes grim behind the thin lenses of her glasses. The eyes that watched her progress slid away as she tried to meet their condemning glances, and it took all her strength and determination not to quicken her normally long strides to reach the haven of her office—the office that was no longer hers.

The long wide hallways were proving endless, and far more crowded than usual, she noticed miserably. Word must have traveled fast about the disgraced researcher. How would they react, she wondered briefly, if she turned to them and announced her innocence? Supposing she stopped dead still, climbed on a convenient soapbox, and declaimed, "Look, it wasn't me who falsified those test results. I wouldn't do such a thing—the experiments mean too much to me. It was your precious Dr. Alleyn, the second in command of this fancy research facility. Dr. Alleyn with the spotless reputation, with the greedy hands, who couldn't bear the thought that his results weren't coming out the way he had planned, who was so convinced that he had to be right that he faked the information on the charts, and then, when it became apparent he was going to get caught, framed me. Framed me because I was the only other person who had access to those records, and because I wouldn't let him put his soft wet hands all over me. Dr. Stanley

Alleyn of the international reputation and the God complex did it, not a silly, trusting, idealistic research assistant one year out of graduate school.''

But Cassie said nothing, increasing her hurried pace down the endless halls.

''For heaven's sake, don't run,'' a soft voice hissed in her ear as Eliza Barnett, her housemate and close friend, caught up with her and threaded her arm through Cassie's, patting her hand reassuringly. ''And don't take these idiots' reactions seriously. Anyone who knows you knows that Alleyn's accusations are ridiculous.''

Cassie met Eliza's trusting blue eyes with a relief that threatened to overwhelm her. ''Thank heavens for you, Liz,'' she murmured, slowing her pace a trifle. ''If it weren't for you and Meredith, I don't know what I'd do. Why do people always want to believe the worst of others?''

They were at the compact office space Cassie shared with Meredith Rathburne, and as Eliza closed the smoked-glass door in the face of the curious, condemning onlookers, Cassie sank into her chair in exhausted relief.

''I told you before.'' Eliza perched on the corner of the solid cherry desk and swung one slender ankle back and forth. ''They don't know you. You've been here only a year, Cassie, and you're not terrifically outgoing. Besides, Alleyn's kept you and Meredith pretty much to himself. And you know perfectly well Meredith's a—a demanding sort of friend. Speaking of which, where is she?'' Eliza's blue eyes wandered curiously around the elegant confines that had been allotted to the two junior research assistants—elegant confines that were supported by Rathburne Foundation money, which flowed abundantly and more than assured Meredith Rathburne's continued tenure at the Thompson Nutri-Center, even if she was tainted by association with the miscreant.

"I have no idea." Cassie pushed the straggling wisps of chestnut hair out of her face and began a desultory inventory of her drawers, emptying them of the sundry accumulations of a year's worth of work. "Probably bearding Thompson in his den and threatening all sorts of things, if I know her." She chuckled weakly.

Eliza hopped off the desk and began tossing Cassie's meager belongings into a file storage box after dumping the files in an untidy heap on the floor. "Do you suppose we're being premature? All Meredith has to do is send her brother after them, and they'll back right down. The Nutri-Center might manage without Rathburne money, but it sure wouldn't be as comfortable. No Danish modern furniture, no private jet for the officers. Thompson may very well decide to listen to your side of the story rather than taking Golden Boy's word for it."

Cassie never hesitated. Into the box went her personal possessions: the picture of her parents, taken on the wedding day of a marriage that had lasted barely long enough to produce two female offspring before breaking apart in rage and frustration; two lab coats; a pair of slightly less practical shoes; three novels of a completely frivolous nature; and a bag of makeup seldom used. So much for all the hopes and dreams of a

brilliant career. She would never get another job after
this disgrace, she knew. She might as well kiss seven
years of college good-bye.

"I don't think it will do any good, Liz," she said
gloomily, slamming shut the final drawer and rising
to her full five feet nine and a half inches. "Bran
Rathburne has always been unwilling to involve himself in the workings of the Nutri-Center. Meredith
got the job on her own merits, not by him pulling
strings. All he does is write out the checks, no questions asked, it seems. And Alleyn's their fair-haired
boy. I think Thompson considers him in line for a
Nobel prize in a few years. I'm a bit more expendable."

"I don't know, Cass," Eliza argued, helping her
strip the impressionistic prints from the oystershell
walls. "I'm putting my money on Meredith. She's devoted to you. I've told you before, I think it's a little
creepy. A grown woman, thirty years old if she's a
day, with all the emotional and social maturity of an
eight-year-old. When she's not racing home to Virginia and the bosom of her family, she's following
you around like a lost puppy dog."

"She sees me as a mother image," Cassie admitted
wryly.

"A mother image! You're three years younger than
she is! I don't think it's healthy for her."

"Probably not," Cassie agreed, casting her eyes
around the lavish office for any belonging she might
have overlooked. "I've tried to make her realize that
I'm human, just like everyone else. Far too human, as
a matter of fact. There's nothing I'd like to do more

right now than wrap my fingers around Stanley Alleyn's neck and squeeze. But Meredith doesn't allow for shades of gray. People are either wonderful or wicked. It's an odd thing for someone to have such a frighteningly brilliant scientific mind and still be so incredibly naive...."

"Well, in any case, we can be glad she thinks you're perfection personified. Whether or not her brother has a tendency to interfere, Thompson knows better than to antagonize a member of the Rathburne family. I'm putting my money on her. And if she doesn't turn the trick, I'm lending a hand."

"Please, Liz," Cassie begged. "Don't risk your own career. I really don't think it will do any good. I pleaded, I begged, I reasoned, and it was absolutely no good. Alleyn just kept sitting there, phony outrage all over his face. And there was nothing Thompson could do but fire me, whether he believed me or not."

"Are you giving up, Cassie O'Neill? Because if you are..." Eliza's words trailed off as a small noise interrupted them. Looking up, Cassie saw Meredith Rathburne framed in the open doorway, her stained lab coat frayed at the cuffs, her wispy black hair falling in its usual untidy bundle down her neck, a run in one stocking, and part of the hem of her expensive silk dress coming down.

Typical Meredith, Cassie thought with affectionate exasperation as she moved toward her friend. Only the young Dr. Rathburne would wear designer clothes with the stitching coming out. And then Cassie caught sight of her expression.

The pale, pretty face was whiter than usual, the blue eyes dark and miserable, the unlipsticked mouth trembling slightly. "I thought you were gone already," she said faintly.

A curiously numb feeling began to fill Cassie, wiping away her earlier outrage and indignation. "Without saying good-bye, Meredith?" she murmured, bewildered. "I wouldn't do that."

"You didn't see my note?" Meredith's voice was flat, emotionless.

"No."

"It's on your desk." Without another word she turned to go, leaving Cassie staring after her in shock and dismay.

"Listen here, Meredith Rathburne!" Eliza jumped into the fray, rather like a mother lion defending her poor wounded cub. "How dare you believe those lies Alleyn's been spreading! You were supposed to be her friend. God, you make me sick! You have all the loyalty of a snail. Let me tell you a thing or two, lady. If you think—"

"Liz!" Cassie's voice was low and admonishing. "Leave her alone. It's up to her to believe what she wants to believe. I'm sorry, Meredith."

Those wide, lost blue eyes were filled with tears as they met hers. "How could you, Cassie?" she demanded, and then fled before Cassie could even offer a word in her own defense.

"Well"—Cassie shrugged, heading for her raincoat—"so much for devoted friends and the power of the Rathburne name."

"Well, I'm certainly not going to abandon you!"

Eliza said stoutly. "I'm going to see Thompson, and then I'm going to find little Dr. Rathburne and give her a piece of my mind."

"No, you're not, Liz. There's no need to make a bad situation worse. It won't do any good to confront Thompson. It'll only get you in trouble. And Meredith will realize, sooner or later, that I'm not the heinous criminal she's imagining, and she'll realize it sooner if she's left alone. I'll talk to her later tonight. I'm sure she'll be full of tears and self-recriminations."

"Listen, sweetie, those kind of friends you don't need," Eliza said sternly.

"No, you're probably right. I need friends like you." She managed to give her housemate a shaky smile. "See you at home?"

"You bet. And don't worry about dinner. I'll stop by the deli and bring home some of Mama Cassato's cannelloni. We'll have an incredible carbo feast to drown our sorrows."

"Sounds good," Cassie managed cheerfully enough. "If I'm not there when you get back, I'll be talking with Meredith."

"Hmmph!" Eliza snorted.

But it soon appeared that Meredith wasn't to be placated. When Cassie reached the small farmhouse outside of Princeton that she and Eliza rented, Meredith was gone from her Carnegie Lake condominium. Dozens of phone calls later Cassie gave up. Either Meredith would initiate contact or not. At this point there was nothing more she could do. She was hardly going to try calling her in Virginia, at the home of the

Nutri-Center's largest contributor. They'd probably slam the phone down the moment she gave her name.

Instead, she put the distressing worry about Meredith to one side and devoted her attention to cannelloni, far too much red wine, and Eliza's increasingly elaborate plans for vindication and revenge. By the time she stumbled into bed the only thought of Meredith was a distant, nagging little worry, greatly overshadowed by more immediate concerns, such as how would she eat, pay her rent, and expose Dr. Stanley Alleyn for the conscienceless skunk he was. Eliza's last plan before retiring had been vague, involving thumbscrews and the rack. Cassie fell asleep with those pleasant visions in her wine-fuzzed brain.

Chapter Two

But there was no wine to fuzz her brain right now, she thought, casting a surreptitious glance at the man beside her as they sped along the Virginia countryside at dizzying speeds.

The silence between them was both an irritant and curiously soothing, though there was nothing the slightest bit soothing about his chiseled profile. There was no softness to Bran Rathburne, no compassion, no tenderness visible there—just a cold, cruel beauty that left Cassie bewildered. For some totally incomprehensible reason she felt both drawn to him and repulsed, and for not the first time she wished she hadn't put her life in his large well-shaped hands, hadn't given in to his demands and come down here. Though, in truth, he hadn't given her much choice.

"Your pilot followed your instructions perfectly," she said finally when she could endure the silence no longer.

"Did he?" He didn't bother to take his eyes from the road, for which Cassie could only be grateful, considering the speed at which they were traveling.

"I think he managed to hit every air pocket on a relatively windless day, and every pothole on the landing strip, besides."

A small infuriating smile tugged at the corner of his mouth. "Don't you like to fly, Ms. O'Neill?" he purred.

"Not anymore." The smile blossomed into an evil chuckle, and Cassie decided silence was a better idea. Moodily she stared out at the lush landscape, at least two weeks further into spring than the New Jersey weather, and determined not to open her mouth again.

How in the world had he managed to get her to come? she wondered again. Was there any way she could have avoided being trapped with this furious stranger beside her? She should have known the suddenly hostile gods—those who had showered her with brains, a fair amount of beauty, and a gift for friendship—would keep up their recent nasty tricks. The fact that it was her twenty-eighth birthday should have warned her, rather than lulled her trusting mind.

She had almost missed the importance of the day. Nursing a cup of strong black coffee, she had ignored the telephone's incessant demands. Perhaps subconsciously she'd known the trouble it would bring, she thought wryly. If only she hadn't given in.

As the insistent ringing died away Cassie looked up at the calendar with a sudden start. May second. It was her twenty-eighth birthday, and she'd almost forgotten it completely. Not that she had much to celebrate, she decided. She was twenty-eight years old, with too

much education, too little experience, a reputation
tarnished beyond repair, no family other than a sister
three thousand miles away, no lovers, and while her
friends had been outraged and supportive, there was
little they could do to help. To top it all off the engine
in her ancient VW had seized, leaving her without
transportation and little money to remedy the situation.

"You, my dear, are a mess," she informed herself
wryly, refilling her coffee cup and offering a silent
toast to her reflection in the small mirror narcissistic
Eliza kept over the sink. "This calls for a celebration." After raiding the refrigerator, she emerged
with a rich coffee cake drenched in sugary icing—the
sort of thing she usually avoided. She had a certain
pride in her tall, slender, almost boyish figure that was
more important to her than sweets. Besides, her work
at Nutri-Center had hardly been conducive to junk
foods.

She cut herself a slice that fully equaled a third of
the cake, sat down, and contemplated her less-than-
bright future.

She was about to cut herself a second slice when the
telephone once more began its incessant demands.
Cassie considered ignoring it, then shrugged. After
all, it might be her sister calling to wish her a happy
birthday, or some long-lost friend offering her a job
and a life of security. And the moon might be made of
green cheese.

"Hello?" Her voice came out husky and slightly
breathless from gulping down that last large piece of
coffee cake.

"Cassandra O'Neill?" The voice didn't request, it demanded, and Cassie felt her hackles rise. The voice was a curious combination of silk and steel, rough demand and velvet softness.

"Speaking." Her voice managed to sound clipped through the final crumbs, her fingers tapping nervously on the table in front of her. She had the vague feeling she wasn't going to like this phone call, and she knew for certain she didn't like the man connected to that enticing voice on the other end of the line. It certainly didn't sound like a singing telegram.

"This is Bran Rathburne." His voice was equally clipped, but an ice-cold rage communicated itself quite effectively. "Do you have any idea what you have done to my sister?"

A fresh wave of guilty concern washed over her at his abrupt words. "What do you mean?" she demanded. "I didn't do a thing to your sister."

"Then why is she lying in a hospital bed, refusing to eat, refusing the operation that is of paramount importance, and moaning about how she failed you in your hour of need?" The voice was bitter and sarcastic, the words flaying her.

"What's she doing in the hopital?" Cassie asked in a more subdued voice. "The last time I saw her she was fine."

"She was in a car accident."

"Oh, no." All Cassie's morbid fantasies had come true. Sweet, vulnerable Meredith's needless disappointment had upset her enough to send her tearing off into the night in that overpowered monstrosity....

"Why the hell did you buy her such a powerful

car?'' was the first thing that came to her lips. "You
should have known she couldn't handle something
like that.''

"I hardly think that's the question right now, Miss
O'Neill.''

"Ms. O'Neill," she corrected instinctively. "When
did it happen? How is she? Will there be any perma-
nent damage? Will she live?''

"I can answer all your questions when you get
down here, Ms. O'Neill.'' His voice was heavily sarcastic.

"Get down there?'' she echoed stupidly. "What
good could I possibly do? I'm not even sure she'll
want to see me.''

"I have my doubts, but her doctor insists that she
won't begin to recover until she clears things up with
you. I'm at my wits' end, willing to try anything. But
let me warn you, *Ms.* O'Neill, that if you say or do
anything to upset her further, I will personally wring
your neck. Is that understood?''

It was all Cassie could do to keep from snapping
back at the hostile, overbearing tone of voice. "How
is she?'' She repeated her earlier question.

"Weak, depressed, and in pain. Her leg was broken
in the accident, and it's not setting properly. They
need to operate and reset it, but she's refusing. If she
doesn't give permission soon, she'll be crippled for
the rest of her life.''

"But isn't there anyone there—''

"There's no one, Ms. O'Neill. There's me and her
ex-fiancé, Gary Leverage, who'd do just about anything for her. And there's not a damn thing we can

do." The desperation in his voice broke through some of her animosity. "She needs you. She says you're the closest thing to a mother she's ever had, and she betrayed you. I would have said the shoe's on the other foot. Some mother image," he snorted, and Cassie's slight warming dissipated.

"I'll call her—"she began, but he broke in.

"You'll come down here," he corrected, his voice accepting no excuses. "You know as well as I that Meredith won't use the telephone. And you'll be here today, if I have to come up and kidnap you personally. You've done Meredith enough harm already. You damn well aren't going to abandon her when she needs you."

"But I can't just leave everything," she protested weakly, knowing she would go.

"Come off it, Ms. O'Neill. You were rightfully dismissed from your job, and with that kind of blot on your record I sincerely doubt that you've found other employment."

"But my car ... the engine seized," she said helplessly. "I could see if I could catch a train—"

"I'm prepared for more excuses," he broke in again, and Cassie's dislike solidified into a heavy core of hatred. "A taxi will be at your house at precisely twelve thirty. He'll drive you to Mercer Airport, where my private plane will be waiting to bring you to Landover. I'll meet you there."

"But—I don't like to fly," she managed. Terrified at the thought was a bit more accurate, but she refused to appear vulnerable before his biting, sarcastic voice.

"Tough. You'll have to grin and bear it, Ms. O'Neill," he shot back. "Be prepared to stay several days—I'm not letting you go till Meredith's well on the way to recovery."

"You'll get me a hotel room?" She tacitly agreed.

"You'll be staying with me. There are over fifteen rooms, and I doubt we'll get in each other's way. I'll meet you at the airport, and we'll go straight to the hospital. The sooner you tell Meredith you forgive her, the sooner she'll start to mend."

"But—I don't think I should stay at your house," she stammered, feeling uncommonly adolescent and gauche.

"Why ever not?" His impatience was clear.

"Because, well, I mean—Meredith never mentioned that you were married, and—" Never had she been so tongue-tied, but somehow the sheer force of the man's personality over the telephone had the ability to intimidate her. Resolutely she pulled herself together. "I don't think it would look good for an unmarried man and an unmarried woman to share a house." She managed a brisk, businesslike tone that sounded unbearably priggish. Appearances were actually the least of her worries. She simply didn't want to spend more time in the company of that man than she could help.

A rude snort of disbelief greeted her protest. "Don't be ridiculous. I find it highly unlikely that I would be unable to control my lustful passions with a woman of your age. Besides, I dislike you intensely for what you did to my sister. You may rest assured, Ms. O'Neill, that your elderly celibacy is safe with me." The phone slammed down, leaving Cassie staring at the receiver in total disbelief.

"Elderly celibacy?" she echoed in amazement. Either Bran Rathburne was extremely young, or he must for some reason imagine her to be on the far side of mature. It was little wonder, with a thirty-year-old woman looking to her for mothering, but nevertheless twenty-seven—no, twenty-eight—was just not that old. That incredibly stupid, overbearing...

Briefly she cast her mind back to the few things Meredith had mentioned about Bran Rathburne, head of the small, but prestigious Rathburne Foundation. He was older than his sister by several years—probably in his mid-thirties—never married, devoted to business and his sister. Cassie could see him now: thinning hair, growing paunch, soft white hands, a fondness for fluffy white cats, with a malicious tongue, besides. Yes, she'd undoubtedly be very safe from his type, but it would still prove a small measure of revenge when he met her and found she wasn't quite the senior citizen he imagined. Cassie found herself looking forward to it.

Well, so much for fantasy, she now thought wearily, grabbing hold of the armrest as her hostile driver took a corner far too quickly. Instead of the sniping eunuch she'd halfway expected, she was confronted with more man than she'd seen in a long, long time. Though doubtless, considering the strong dislike that already ran between them, she was just as safe. That thought should have reassured her. For some reason it had the opposite effect.

Chapter Three

They sped farther and farther into the countryside, the more populated areas fading in the distance. The leaves were just out, in that full, young green that had always captivated Cassie. She tried to concentrate on the beauty of the late Virginia springtime, ignoring her chauffeur. It was fully twenty minutes of silence later when he turned onto a winding, perfectly maintained driveway, past open iron gates, and another five minutes after that when he pulled up in front of a huge rambling farmhouse-type structure that clearly dated from the last century.

Bran pulled to a stop with a screeching of tires, turning off the motor with an abrupt jerk. For the first time since they'd set off on their mad dash across the countryside he turned to stare at her, his mirrored sunglasses giving her no clue to thoughts that were doubtless uncomplimentary.

"I presume this isn't the hospital?" She finally broke the silence. "I thought we were going to visit Meredith right away."

"You thought wrong. I'm not about to let you talk to her until we come to an understanding."

"Do you suppose this could wait a bit?" she asked wearily, stalling for time. The close confines of the Jaguar only heightened her awareness of his very potent maleness, and she wanted nothing more than to escape from his presence for a few brief minutes to try to regain some sense of equilibrium. Never in her life had she reacted to a man this way, with an absurd combination of hostility and desire; she was used to men as friends or casual dates. Since a short, disastrous love affair in her mid-twenties she had preferred it that way, keeping eligible men at a friendly distance. She knew far too well how easy it was to get hurt. But this was something new and bewildering, and she needed time and distance to compose herself. "I've had less than a comfortable trip. I would really appreciate a cup of tea and a chance to relax before we get into a battle royal."

"And what makes you think it's going to be a battle royal?" He pushed the sunglasses onto his forehead, his most powerful weapon—those incredible eyes—watching her closely.

"Is there really any doubt?" she countered, reaching for the door handle, knowing full well he could stop her if he wanted to.

"Not much," he agreed, swinging out of his side of the car and watching her wrestle once more with the duffel bag with an unmoved expression. "I'll show you to your room."

"Is that necessary?" She followed him up the

broad front steps, a part of her admiring the old
brickwork beneath her feet and the freshly painted
stucco on the front of the old farmhouse. "Couldn't
one of your staff do it? I mean, I assume you have
housekeepers and maids and such. I can't see you
doing housework." *Score one for me,* she thought
cheerfully.

A momentary flash of amusement crossed his dark
face, followed by an evil little grin. "I have a house-
keeper-cook who comes in during the days, Ms.
O'Neill, and two cleaning ladies who come in twice a
week. But there is no live-in staff. You'll be here all
alone with me."

Score one for him, she thought. Swallowing, Cassie
followed him to the front door. "Ah, but you've already assured me that my elderly celibacy would remain intact."

"Oh, don't worry. You'll be completely safe from
me," he said with just a trace too much alacrity, his
eyes sweeping over her with studied sensual arrogance.

"I had little doubt of that," she replied with as
much dignity as she could muster, slinging the bag
over her shoulder and following him out of the bright
sunlight into the darkened entryway.

Considering his rampant antagonism, Cassie would
have been far happier if the inside of his eighteenth-
century farmhouse was a sterile abomination. She
should have known better. Despite the raw dislike between the two of them, everything about him, including his home, was far too attractive to her. The long,
random-width oak flooring shone with loving care,

and the several Oriental carpets scattered on its shiny surface were very old and very beautiful. Each piece of furniture was a piece of history, the white plaster walls were at least a foot thick, and doubtless the fireplace was a working one.

Bran Rathburne, however, barely gave her time to absorb all these treasures before he started up the wide winding staircase to the second floor. A perfect staircase for a bride to soar down, or a girl making her debut, she thought, her mind on Meredith. Perhaps a more conciliatory tone might help with her reluctant host.

"Meredith must have loved growing up here," she offered tentatively, panting somewhat in her effort to keep up with Bran's long strides. The duffel bag kept slipping off her shoulders, one of her hairpins was falling out, and her feet hurt.

"You're under a misapprehension, Ms. O'Neill. This isn't the Rathburne family home. That was left to my father's second wife, who promptly sold it. Neither Meredith nor I cared to live with her."

No love lost there, Cassie noted. And score another point for Bran Rathburne. She couldn't attribute the wonderful combination of elegance, comfort, and history to his mother, and she knew only too well that Meredith had no interest whatsoever in her surroundings. "But this is Meredith's home?" she persisted, huffing slightly.

"For the last twelve years," he agreed, halting in front of a white doorway with a shiny brass knob. "I bought it just after our father died. This is your room," he added abruptly. "The bathroom's across the hallway. When you've rested sufficiently, you can meet me downstairs in the study, and I'll provide you with a cup of tea—and a few rules and regulations to govern your behavior with my sister." Without even bothering to open the door he turned on his heels and started back down the hall.

"But—how will I find you?" she queried. "This house is immense, you realize."

The smile he cast back at her could almost be described as wolfish. "Just keep opening doors until you find me."

It took Cassie less time than she anticipated to get settled into the large, comfortable room Bran Rathburne had reluctantly allotted her. The patchwork quilt on the antique spool bed was obviously an heirloom, and the French doors that looked out on a veranda that ran the length of the house let in a glorious amount of sunlight. Rest and relaxation eluded her as she thought of the dark, disapproving man downstairs. It would have been so much easier if he had been the aging mama's boy she had anticipated. And why had she expected him to be? Rathburne was known at the Nutri-Center as a perceptive and somewhat ruthless benefactor, an astute businessman, and nobody's fool. Perhaps she'd been misled by Meredith's glowing adoration. Somehow Cassie had reasoned that a man devoted to his sister and still unmarried in his mid-thirties must somehow be less than masculine. Combine that with an anticipated resemblance to the somewhat eccentric Meredith, and it was not unexpected that Cassie would jump to the same erroneous conclusions that Rathburne himself had. He was as effeminate and eccentric as Cassie was elderly. But God, it would have made things easier if he had been.

By the time she'd shed her heavier outer sweater, smoothed her coronet of chestnut braids, and splashed some cold water on her makeup-free face, a good half hour had passed. For a moment Cassie considered stalling, letting him stew downstairs in his study for just a bit longer, but it was already nearing five o'clock, and Cassie was determined to see Meredith as soon as the autocrat would let her. The sooner she saw Meredith and calmed the woman's apprehensions, the sooner Cassie could escape back to Princeton. The more she thought of her host, the more determined she was to make her getaway. Despite Bran's obvious dislike of her, there was a trace of something in those unfathomable eyes that called to her—a call she was determined not to heed.

It took her longer than she had expected to find the study. She stumbled into the kitchen, a formal dining room, a breakfast room, two living rooms, and a bathroom before finally coming upon Rathburne's disapproving stare from behind a beautiful old mahogany partners' desk. "I can see I judged you accurately," he observed, and his tone suggested, not for the first time. "The tea is just ready." He leaned back in his chair, eyes hooded, fingertips together in a meditative gesture. "Are you going to just stand in the door like a frightened rabbit?"

That galvanized her. Straightening her shoulders, she strode into the room, took the pottery mug with its steaming brew, and sat down opposite him, her eyes clear and hostile. "Hardly a frightened rabbit, Mr. Rathburne," she snapped.

"Bran," he corrected absently, stirring his own tea.

"Mr. Rathburne," she repeated stubbornly.

"I think not. That's the first thing we have to discuss, Cassie. I think it goes without saying that you dislike me as much as I dislike you. But our personal animosity will do nothing to help Meredith's state of mind. As a matter of fact, quite the opposite. For some unfathomable reason you are almost as important to her as I am."

"How very odd," Cassie broke in icily.

"Odd, indeed. But no one has ever said that Meredith had sensible tastes. Gifted children quite often grow up to be disturbed adults."

For a moment Cassie was speechless with outrage. "Why, you—you utter bastard," she sputtered. "How dare you say such a thing about Meredith? She's no more disturbed than—than I am. Just because she doesn't quite conform to society's mold of what a proper young lady should be doesn't mean she's disturbed! How could you...!" She let the words trail off before the suddenly genuine smile that lit his face.

"Well, I'm pleased to see that got a rise out of you faster than anything else so far. So you must care about my sister, at least to some extent."

"Of course I care about her! Why do you think I'm here?"

"Because I didn't give you any choice?" he suggested.

"Believe me, Mr. Rathburne, if I didn't want to

come and see Meredith, nothing on earth would have got me here."

"That's debatable, but hardly the point," he said wearily. "And the name is Bran. As far as Meredith is concerned—and, indeed, anyone else you happen to meet while you're here—you and I are friends. I don't want Meredith to have any further troubles, worrying about whether the two of us are getting along. Her last few visits were all full of how wonderful you were, how certain she was that I'd adore you." There was a faint grimace at such an absurd thought. "I don't want to disappoint her."

"So when I see her, I'm supposed to pretend that we're great friends? I don't know if I'm that good an actress."

"I have faith in you, Cassie. I'm sure you're capable of all sorts of duplicity. I've already informed my stepmother that you're here to see Meredith and planning to stay at least two weeks. By tomorrow everyone will know." The sneer was back, this time not for her. "Dear Ellen has one of the best rumor networks I know of."

"Two weeks?" Cassie echoed. "I can't stay here that long. I have to get back to Princeton."

"Why?"

"For one thing, I'm out of a job, in case you've forgotten."

"I'm hardly likely to forget such a thing. If you hadn't been caught in time, the disgrace would have discredited Dr. Thompson, the Nutri-Center, the Rathburne Foundation, and everything connected with them. I think it unlikely you're going to find any work in the near future. And if you leave here before I'm entirely ready to let you go, you'll find that you won't get work anywhere—not as a cocktail waitress, not as a laundress, not as a garbageman. Believe me.''

Cassie had never seen anyone look quite so ruthless. "I do," she replied in a husky whisper, mesmerized. She quickly abandoned any plan to protest her innocence to this suddenly frightening man. It would obviously be a waste of breath.

"Good." He rose to his full height, towering over her seated figure, determined to intimidate her further. She knew she should rise also, to try to diminish his demoralizing effect, but for the moment she felt quite unable to move. "There's another side to this, of course. If you play along with me, are pleasant with my friends, and reassure Meredith, then I'll make it worth your while. Your money must be running low at this point. You can consider your two weeks here a job."

That was enough to make her shoot to her feet. "And you can go to hell. I'm here to see if I can help Meredith, because I care about her. But I am certainly not going to take any of your filthy money. You may think money buys everything, Bran Rathburne, but you're wrong. I'm not for sale and I'm not here to be threatened, either. I'm here because I want to be, and you can take your money and shove it."

"Whoa!" He stared at her, obviously perplexed. "Very well, then, no money. But I could see about your finding another job. Would that be acceptable to someone of such obviously high moral principles?" His expression made it more than clear how dubious he considered her moral principles to be.

She would have liked to have taken that offer and thrown it back in his handsome face, but reason prevailed. "Perhaps," she said stiffly.

"And you'll be charming and friendly in front of Meredith and our friends? Not say anything to upset her further?" He hesitated. "Please?" That last effort must have cost him dearly, for he fairly ground it out.

"Aren't you afraid she won't know me if I'm too nice?"

"I'm willing to take that chance." His voice was grim. "Is it a deal?"

"I suppose so." She tossed it off, heading for the door. "I'm ready to see Meredith. Can we go?"

He was at the door before her, one iron hand capturing the soft flesh of her upper arm, the fingers biting in. It was all Cassie could do to keep from crying out, but she looked way, way up into his face with all the calm she could muster.

"I hope I can trust you." His voice was low and honey sweet and appallingly seductive. Cassie swallowed once. "Because you will find I can be a very dangerous enemy. We're forced to deal together, Ms. Cassie O'Neill, much as I dislike the necessity. Play me false, say one thing wrong to Meredith, and you'll regret it for the rest of your life."

He was standing so close to her, she could feel the heat emanating from his body, smell the faint, enticing smell of his spicy after-shave and pure, raw masculinity. By moving a few inches she could rest her head against that leanly muscled shoulder, feel his heart beating beneath her ear, he was so damn close. And she must be going out of her mind, she thought.

"I might have a hard time explaining the bruises on my arm," she said with an admirable attempt at calm, determined not to show either fear or the other, more overpowering emotion he elicited from her.

Bran's other hand had reached up and caught her chin, the long fingers resting lightly on her determined jawline. "You'd have an even harder time explaining a black eye," he murmured, his breath warm and sweet on her upturned face. He stared down at her for a long moment, his eyes watching as she involuntarily ran the tip of her tongue over suddenly dry lips. "I wish I knew whether I could trust you" he said, half to himself, his tight grip on her arm loosening somewhat.

"You're going to have to" was all she said.

"I suppose I really have no choice whatsoever, do I?" He released her arm, and as the blood rushed back through it, she stumbled slightly. He reached out to steady her, but she flung off his arm.

"We only have to be friends in public," she stated, more shaken than she'd care to admit by his nearness. "I'll meet you at the car."

Chapter Four

Her first sight of Meredith was enough to knock all the fight out of her. Bran had preceded her into the room, reappearing a moment later. "She's asleep," he said in a low, husky voice. "I don't know if we ought to wake her. Why don't you come in for just a moment? She's pretty heavily sedated. If she woke up, she might not even recognize us."

"You still haven't told me the extent of her injuries." Cassie hesitated. The smell of the hospital, the faint, muffled sounds of electronic life-support systems, and the hurried, no-nonsense tread of rubber-soled nurses, all brought back horrifying memories she'd much rather do without. She'd always had a horror of hospitals, due, no doubt, to a traumatic tonsillectomy at age six. Ever since then that hospital smell had sent her into a panic. A part of her backed away, involuntarily, her eyes wide and frightened behind the lenses of her glasses. "She's going to die, isn't she?" There was a numb misery in her voice, and Bran looked at her strangely.

"What's gotten into you?" His voice was brusque.

"No, she's not going to die. Not if I can help it. She's got several broken ribs, a moderate concussion, a bruised liver and a kidney, and then there's her leg, which needs an operation. But there's nothing terminal. She's surprisingly tough physically, even if emotionally she's at the mercy of—" For some reason he bit back the no-doubt highly unflattering description of Cassie. "She'll make it just fine, but she'll make it a little faster if she feels you've forgiven her."

"But if she's been here for two weeks and is still under heavy sedation..." Cassie moaned.

"Two weeks? Whatever made you think she'd been here that long?" His impatience was on a very tight rein. "She's only been in here a few days. She had the accident Sunday afternoon. Where did you get the idea that she's been here longer?"

"I—I don't know. I just assumed she'd had a smashup on the way down here from Princeton that night." She swallowed, asking the question she'd dreaded to ask but had to know. "How did it happen?"

There was a slight softening in Bran's hard features, and the silver-blue eyes beneath the winged brows were suddenly almost kind. "You thought you were to blame for that, too, didn't you?" he questioned with sudden insight. "That you upset Meredith so much, she'd gotten in an accident as she rushed home, is that it?"

There was a note in his usually harsh voice that almost might be called compassionate, and Cassie felt herself blossoming beneath it. She nodded.

"She had the accident Sunday afternoon, ten days

after she got back here. It was entirely the other
driver's fault, and there was no way she could have
avoided it, no matter how stable her state of mind
was. Does that help?''

''Yes,'' she said, smiling up at him gratefully, a
huge weight of guilt dropping from her slender
shoulders. For a moment he smiled down at her, and
then the small moment passed, his brows snapped
together, and his eyes grew wintry once more.

''Which doesn't absolve you of your responsi-
bility,'' he growled. ''She had spent the last ten
days moping and weeping and wandering around the
house. She broke off her engagement to Gary Leverage, which was about the best thing she had going for
her, and you could just as easily have been responsi-
ble for the car accident, which has left her bedridden
and racked with pain. So don't think you're off the
hook, Ms. O'Neill.''

Several infuriated retorts sprang to her lips just as
the door opened and a nurse appeared to beckon them
in. It was Cassie's first audience, and she decided to
make full use of it. She smiled up at Bran, a breathtakingly beautiful smile, and threaded her arm through
his. ''I think Meredith's awake now, Bran,'' she
cooed. ''And, please, call me Cassie. I know Meredith
would want us to be dear, good friends.'' She included
the obviously fascinated nurse in her friendly smile,
and she could feel Bran's muscles tense in obvious
frustration, but there was nothing he could do—he
had set the rules of the game. So he smiled down at
her, the smile curving his sensuous mouth, but stopping short of his glorious eyes, and his hand reached

out to pat her arm reassuringly. If the pat was slightly heavier-handed than one would expect—well, who was to know?

"Cassie," he agreed smoothly.

All secret amusement vanished from Cassie as she surveyed the still figure of her friend. Intravenous feeding tubes were draped from one arm, her head was bandaged, and her eyes were closed, sunken, and bruised. Her left leg was propped and swathed, and her breathing was the shallow, slow breathing of one deeply drugged.

"What in the world is she on?" Cassie demanded of Bran in an urgent whisper.

"Painkillers. The leg is pretty agonizing, according to Dr. Haughey, and the ribs and bruised organs are no trip to Hollywood, either. Don't worry. They're being careful. They don't want to compound Meredith's problems by adding drug addiction to them."

Cassie nodded, tears filling her eyes. "Is she still asleep?"

"She drifts in and out," the nurse replied. "I'm sure if you felt like talking to her, it would be a good thing. She's been asleep for quite a while now."

Slowly, reluctantly, Cassie let go of Bran's arm, which had somehow become a lifeline, and moved closer to the bed. The supine figure remained motionless, and tentatively Cassie put a gentle hand on Meredith's bruised, lifeless one.

"Meredith?" she whispered softly.

Slowly the bruised eyelids fluttered open. "Cassie?" she breathed, unbelieving. "Cassie, is it really you?"

It took Cassie a moment to get her voice under control. "Of course it is, you ninny," she said with her usual affectionate gruffness. "I came as soon as I heard—wild horses couldn't have kept me away. How did you get yourself into this mess?"

Meredith managed a crooked smile. "Just lucky, I guess," she whispered. "I never knew what hit me."

"I guess not. Listen, sweetie, I want you to rest and take care of yourself. Your brother told me some garbage about you refusing to have your leg operated on. Now, you're old enough and smart enough to know better. You'll have an awfully hard time moving about the laboratory in a wheelchair."

Meredith's face crumpled. "But I don't have a job anymore, Cassie. I quit after they fired you. I realized— Oh, Cassie, can you ever forgive me for doubting you? I should have known...." Tears were streaming down her pale, bruised face, and Cassie placed a gently restraining hand on her mouth.

"Hush, now. It wasn't your fault. How were you to know?"

"But I should have trusted you," Meredith wailed, a spasm of pain crossing her face. "I know you too well to have thought you capable of such a thing."

"And I know you too well to have taken your momentary doubts seriously. I tore up your note and forgot about it."

"But Eliza didn't," Meredith said stubbornly. "She wrote me and said—and said—"

"Forget about Eliza," Cassie ordered, mentally cursing her over-solicitous roommate. "We've all been upset over this business at the Nutri-Center. I'm sure she didn't mean whatever she said."

"Oh, but she did!" Meredith insisted. "And I de-

served it—every word. But when I get better, I'll
make it up to you. I have money, Cassie. We'll start
our own research laboratory, and we won't have to
answer to anybody. I've already told Gary that I can't
possibly marry him. I'll be too busy, and—"

"Hush," Cassie said again, doing her best not to
show the absolute horror she felt at Meredith's mu-
nificent plan. Being subsidized by her rich friend was
the last thing in the world she wanted or would accept.
"We'll talk about that later. In the meantime, I think
you should get more rest."

Meredith's clawlike hand reached out and caught
hers. "You'll come back to see me?" she begged.
"You won't go back to Princeton right away?"

"No, Meredith, I'll be staying. As a matter of fact,
your brother is putting me up for a couple of weeks.
He very kindly called me and invited me down to see
you." She made a tiny hidden gesture for Bran to present himself at the bedside, and a moment later she
felt his presence behind her, his hand strong and
warm on her shoulder.

"Hi, babe," he said softly. "How are you doing?"

"Okay, now that Cassie's here. You like her, don't
you, Bran?" she begged, her voice a reedy sound in
the stillness of the room.

The hand tightened on Cassie's shoulder. "Of
course I do, babe. How could I help myself?" he said
easily, and Cassie could only marvel at what a consummate actor he was. With his large hand warm and
strong on her shoulder, his voice soft and caressing,
she could almost imagine he did like her, even cared
for her. It was lucky she was strong-minded enough to

remember the cold contempt that lit his eyes when he looked down at her. She wasn't so easily fooled.

However, Bran's playacting had the desired effect on his audience. Meredith's pale face took on a warm glow that betrayed her matchmaking tendencies, and the nurse behind them sighed a small, romantic sigh. It was all Cassie could do not to shake off that comforting, restraining hand, but she couldn't erase that hopeful glow on her friend's battered countenance.

"We'll be back tomorrow, Meredith," she said, slowly detaching her hand from her weak grasp.

"Both of you?"

"Both of us," she agreed. "Maybe not together, but—"

"Together," Meredith demanded with more than a trace of petulance.

"But your brother must have certain plans, responsibilities..." she began weakly, and the hand on her shoulder pressed down warningly.

"Together," Bran agreed smoothly, steering her away from the bedside.

The trip back to the house was conducted in a strained silence. Bran made no move to break it, and Cassie was too caught up in a thousand thoughts and worries to make an effort. It was past eight and almost dark when they pulled up in front of the rambling farmhouse. This time he made no effort to cut the motor, and in the twilight confines of the Jaguar his chiseled face looked cold and distant.

"Mrs. Bellingson will have gone for the day. I'm sure you can find something for supper in the kitchen—help yourself." His voice couldn't have sounded less accommodating.

"Aren't you coming in?" She managed to keep her voice cool and disinterested.

"No." That was fairly definite.

"All right." She reached for the handle of the door, but before she could open it, his arm shot out and stopped her. There was no mistaking it, she realized sadly. He was in a towering rage.

"Tell me, Cassie O'Neill," he demanded softly, his face very close to hers in the darkened car, "did you really think you'd get away with it?"

For a moment she was nonplussed. "Get away with what?"

"With wrapping Meredith around your little finger. With playing on her vulnerability and guilt to set you up in your own cushy laboratory. Didn't you realize she has trustees and people who care about her, who make sure she isn't taken in by vampires like you?"

The expression of disgusted incredulity on her face was enough to penetrate even his infuriated abstraction. "You really believe that, don't you?" She managed to keep her voice low and even.

"You've run true to form so far."

There was nothing she could say, no defense she could offer. He would believe what he wished to believe. He was already convinced that she'd committed the most unspeakable of crimes in the field of research—falsified data—and he somehow thought she had, with Machiavellian cunning, managed to get his sister under her thumb and take advantage of her trusting nature. Now he was sure she was trying to bilk Meredith of her rather substantial fortune. It was a wonder he could stand having her in the same house.

But then, obviously, he couldn't. His eyes were cold in the twilight. Cassie stared at him, too weary to argue further, or to even attempt to defend herself.

"Think what you want to," she said. "I'm too tired and too disinterested in your opinion to bother arguing with you tonight. Will you remove your arm?" She stared at it pointedly, unable to move with him barring her way. "And then you can go off to whatever poor fool is enjoying your favor at the moment. Believe me, she has all my sympathy. And I can get something to eat and a good night's sleep."

His arm withdrew, his hand accidently brushing her small, high breasts. Both of them jerked apart as if burned, and then Bran managed a shaky laugh. "You needn't worry, Cassie. We've already agreed that your elderly celibacy is safe from my scheming. I'll make do with the poor fool awaiting me."

Without another word she opened the door and scrambled out of the car. The Jaguar pulled away with a sudden roar and a spurt of gravel, and Cassie watched it leave with mixed emotions. Never had she undergone so many different feelings in twenty-four hours. Fortunately, the absent Mrs. Bellingson had left a scattering of lights lit about the rambling old farmhouse, and it was with no great difficulty that Cassie found her way to the back kitchens.

She ate her dinner in solitary splendor—a satisfying repast of cold chicken, spinach salad, hot rolls, and a very nice white wine, followed by fresh strawberries with thick whipped cream. Mrs. Bellingson had left enough chicken for two, but by the time Cassie was finished there was none left. She had had nothing but coffee cake for breakfast, and tea with honey since then. A hell of a way to spend her birthday, she thought, toasting her reflection and draining her glass. Thank heavens, she assured herself, that Bran Rathburne had something better to do with his time. The thought of sharing a table with that astoundingly handsome, unsettlingly disapproving gentleman was the last thing she wanted tonight of all nights.

By nine o'clock the exhaustion and wine had hit her like a sledgehammer, but she was determined not to succumb. She would find a television set, she decided, and find something worth watching. Or, even better, a stereo. She could put something very sophisticated and cynical and sad on the turntable, curl up on a comfortable sofa with a glass of brandy, and shed a few easy tears. She was not going to bed at nine o'clock on her twenty-eighth birthday.

The stereo was ensconced behind cherry paneled cupboards in the smaller of the two living rooms. Conveniently nearby, as if she had ordered them from a capricious fate, were a brandy decanter and a tray of snifters, a comfortable blue sofa loaded with pillows, and a record collection with a substantial assortment of French chansonniers. Charles Aznavour fit her mood perfectly, and as she fell asleep, the taste of brandy warm and sweet in her mouth, her last thought was of Venice turning blue.

She awoke slowly, reluctantly, for a moment unaware of her surroundings. It was darker than when she had fallen asleep—only one small lamp was lit against the nighttime shadows, and someone had placed an afghan over her sleeping body. The brandy snifter had been removed and the stereo turned off.

She struggled to sit up, peering at her watch through the gloom. A quarter to twelve. She felt as if she had slept for days.

But who could have come in and covered her? she wondered. Certainly not Bran Rathburne. If he'd had his way, he would have done what she'd seen in an old movie—drench her sleeping form with water and then open the windows to let the cold night air speed her on the way to pneumonia. Though she was scarcely likely to develop a chill on a cool May night, she thought.

At the thought of the austere Bran Rathburne sneaking around she giggled, and then realized, despite the massive amounts of food she'd managed to consume a few hours past, she was still hungry. Normally she ignored such midnight cravings, certain that giving in to them would lead her down the road to perdition and double chins, but she still had fifteen minutes left of her birthday, and after such a horrendous day, she deserved some pampering.

Draping the afghan around her tired shoulders, she made her way toward the kitchen, mentally reviewing the contents of the refrigerator as she'd last seen them. There were still strawberries and cream left, though she'd finished the last of the chicken. Perhaps a bowl of cereal with heavy cream...

Pushing open the swinging door, she came to an abrupt stop. Bran was sitting on a tall stool at the counter, a thick sandwich in one hand, a scowl on his

face at the sight of her. His suit coat and vest had been
discarded, and with his white silk shirt rolled up at the
sleeves and unbuttoned halfway down to reveal an enticing triangle of fine hair on his tanned chest, he
looked surprisingly approachable. The tousled black
hair added a rakish touch to him, and Cassie sleepily
shook her head. Despite his human looks, she had to
remember he was about as warm as the yeti.

Her braids had tumbled down past her shoulders,
and it was beyond her to suppress the luxuriant yawn
that blossomed forth.

Bran tried to glare at her. "I thought you were
asleep. What do you want?"

Cassie was too tired to argue. "I *was* asleep. Did
you put the afghan around me? That was very kind of
you."

"I didn't want to face Meredith if you got sick," he
said gruffly. "Why don't you go up to bed?"

"And leave you alone," Cassie finished for him,
yawning again. "I would, but I'm still hungry."

"You couldn't be. You ate both your dinner and
mine," he announced flatly.

"Oh, I'm sorry. I didn't realize you were expecting
to eat when you got back from—from whatever." The
phrase *poor fool* came into her head, and determinedly
she banished it. "Besides, I hadn't eaten anything
since breakfast, so I was hungry. I still am." Sleepily
she wandered over toward the refrigerator, opening
the door and leaning against it dreamily.

Bran stood up, tossing his napkin onto his empty
plate, and walked slowly over to her. With surprising
gentleness he removed the door from her grasp and

shut it. To Cassie's sleep-mazed mind he seemed enormously tall, but for once his size was comforting, not threatening.

She smiled up at him. "Heavens, you're tall," she murmured. "How tall are you?"

"Six feet four." His mouth creased in reluctant amusement. "How much brandy *did* you drink?"

"Just enough." She sighed, leaning back against the refrigerator and staring up at him dreamily.

Almost by its own volition one of his strong tanned hands reached out and caught one of her thick brown braids as it rested against her breast. "You don't look old enough to drink in these." He gave it a gentle tug.

"But I am," she replied, a hazy, distant part of her brain wondering if it was the brandy, or exhaustion, or the heady effect of his nearness that was turning her knees to Jell-o. "I'm twenty-eight years old today. It's my birthday, and no one remembered," she mourned. "At least, it's my birthday for another"—she squinted at the clock on the wall, her glasses having disappeared at some point during the evening, along with her boots—"another four minutes," she finished triumphantly, proud of her recalcitrant vision.

The light that shimmered in his silver-blue eyes should have warned her. "Four minutes," he echoed. "That doesn't give us a great deal of time to celebrate."

"Celebrate?"

His hand reached down and caught her willful chin, tilting her face up to meet his. "I shouldn't do this," he muttered under his breath, his eyes burning into hers. "And I wouldn't, but, like you, I've had too much brandy. And you, my dear Ms. O'Neill, are very intoxicating." His mouth moved slowly closer. "Happy birthday, Cassie."

Slowly, languorously, his mouth met hers, his lips soft, gentle, and oh, so enticing. Shock left Cassie motionless, unresponsive, until he pulled his head away. "That's no way to celebrate your birthday, Cassie," he chided, a light of amusement in his eyes. "Open your mouth for me." And once more he set his mouth on hers, demanding a response she could no longer withhold.

Her mouth opened to receive his questing tongue as her arms found their way around his neck. She felt as if she were drowning beneath the sensual onslaught of that too-experienced mouth with its faint tang of brandy and tobacco, but she was helpless to resist. Her heart was pounding against her rib cage as his mouth trailed soft, hurried little kisses across the bridge of her nose, her delicate jawline, and down her neck. One of those strong beautiful hands of his found its way beneath her turtleneck and was cupping her breast through the lacy scrap of bra, and the tip hardened with sudden, blazing desire.

Once more his mouth caught hers, his tongue making tiny darting forays into enemy territory as his body pressed hers back against the cool metal of the refrigerator door. She could feel the very tangible evidence of his desire against her aching, yearning body, and for the first time in her life she felt herself being swept away by a maelstrom of desires she barely understood. Arching her body up against his hips, she moaned, deep and low in the back of her throat, wanting to get ever closer to his strength.

Bran had managed to unhook the front clasp of her bra beneath the sweater, and his thumb flicked over one sensitized nipple until Cassie thought she would explode. His other hand had moved to the back of her neck, holding her securely in place for his searching, devouring mouth, and suddenly Cassie knew that she was incapable of stopping him. He hated and despised her, thought her capable of the grossest immoralities, and if he wanted, he could have her lying on the kitchen floor in another moment. Desperately she tried to fight her weakness, but she had never felt like this before. There was no way she could fight what was such an overwhelming mystery, no reserves she could call on to defend herself against the sudden onslaught of passion.

And then, suddenly, his mouth left hers, his hand motionless on her breast, as he listened to the grandfather clock in the front hallway strike twelve.

He looked down at her, relief and regret and something else in his eyes. "It's midnight, Cinderella. Go to bed." And with that he released her, turning on his heels and striding out the kitchen door into the spring night without a backward glance, leaving Cassie, a trembling mass of shame, anger, and thwarted desire, leaning up against the refrigerator door, grateful for the support she desperately needed.

Chapter Five

When she awoke late the next morning, her boots and glasses were beside her bed, the afghan, last seen residing on the kitchen floor, folded neatly beside them. Could Bran have come in during the small hours of the morning? she wondered. Somehow the thought of those condemning eyes staring down at her sleeping, defenseless form was highly unsettling. Especially after that kiss that he had regretted even before he instigated it.

A knock on the door broke through her reveries, and before she could reply it opened a crack, revealing a motherly soul with gray hair, bifocals, and a matronly figure covered in a crisp apron. The woman was not likely to be Bran's stepmother, she realized with amusement.

"Mrs. Bellingson?" she ventured, pulling herself upright, breathing a small sigh of relief that she had found enough energy to pull on a warm flannel nightgown before she fell into bed.

The older lady's smile widened, and she pushed the door the rest of the way open with the heavily laden tray she was carrying. "You're up, then, dearie," she observed. "I thought you might be by now. Bran said you had a late night of it and I wasn't to disturb you, but Mr. Leverage is coming by in an hour and a half to take you to see Meredith, and I thought you'd want enough time to have a shower and a decent breakfast. Did you sleep well?" She placed the tray on Cassie's lap, beaming with pride.

Cassie bit back a groan. Fluffy scrambled eggs, sausages, fresh cinnamon buns, orange juice, delicious-smelling coffee—there was more than Cassie usually consumed in a week of breakfasts. "It looks wonderful, Mrs. Bellingson, but I couldn't possibly eat so much." She tried to keep the longing note out of her voice, almost succeeding.

"Nonsense!" she replied firmly. "A body needs a good breakfast if she's to make it through the day. Besides, you could do with a bit of feeding up. You're too skinny."

Her arm sufficiently twisted, Cassie broke off a bun and slathered it with butter. "How would you know I was too skinny?" she queried cheerfully. "You haven't seen me out of bed yet."

"Bran said so," Mrs. Bellingson replied, oblivious to the reaction that artless comment evoked. "He told me I should feed you up. You haven't been getting enough food, living on your own. That's the problem, well I know it. When my daughters moved out, they starved themselves down into skinny little things just like you and stayed that way, until they got married and had their babies. You'll see, the same thing'll happen to you. But in the meantime you need to keep up your strength. You look more like a young boy than a girl.''

"Thanks a lot," she said around her second bun. "Did Bran say that, too?" He hadn't kissed her like she was a young boy. At least, she hoped not.

"No, ma'am. That was my idea. No offense meant, of course." The eyes were anxious behind the distorting bifocals.

"And none taken," Cassie said generously. "Would you care for some coffee?"

"No, dearie, thank you. The doctor only allows me decaffeinated, and that's so weak, it's not worth the bother. Bran also said to tell you he'll see Meredith separately and tell her he's tied up with the Foundation. He probably won't be around for a few days, but you're to make yourself at home. The pool is probably warm enough to swim in by now, and there are books, television, and the like.''

Cassie didn't know whether to be relieved or disappointed. She told herself relief should be foremost, and she favored Mrs. Bellingson with her most ravishing smile. "That should make things very comfortable. But how will I get back and forth from the hospital? I didn't bring my car."

"Mr. Leverage has offered to drive you." Mrs. Bellingson looked slightly unhappy at the thought. "And if there's any way I can make your stay more comfortable..."

"You already have," Cassie assured her. "And Bran won't be home at all for several days?"

"Not so's you'd notice. I'll make your supper and leave it with instructions. Bran will eat out, I expect.

Just pretend he isn't around, and he probably won't be. He and Lucy Barrow spend a lot of time together—not that he shouldn't see through her, knowing who her aunt is." Mrs. Bellingson sniffed disapprovingly.

"All right, I'll bite. Who's her aunt?" The scrambled eggs were perfect, not too wet, not too dry, and Cassie resigned herself to two weeks of uninhibited eating. She could always fast when she got back to Princeton, and her finances would probably appreciate it if she did, she thought.

"The second Mrs. Rathburne, that's who. Bran and Meredith's stepmother, and a social butterfly with the morals of an alley cat, if you ask me, which you didn't. And I should learn to keep my opinions to myself. But, heavens, it does sit hard with me when I think of all the harm she's done those children." Heaving a sigh, the housekeeper headed for the door. "Now, don't you worry about these dishes. I'll come back and get them later. You just enjoy yourself, and I'll give you a call when Mr. Leverage arrives."

Cassie, of course, did no such thing. After a long hot shower, she dressed in tan slacks and a forest-green cotton sweater, made her bed, and carried the tray down to the kitchen. Her head felt heavy beneath the coronet of wet braids, but she didn't have enough time to dry her hair properly first before fixing it, and she wasn't about to float around with a curtain of chestnut locks hanging down her back all day.

"Now, you shouldn't have done that, dearie." Mrs. Bellingson greeted her from the far end of the kitchen, up to her elbows in flour and bread dough. "I

told you I'd get them. I suppose you made your bed,
too."

"I suppose I did." Cassie placed the tray down by
the sink and perched on a kitchen stool. "And I didn't
want you coming to get me when Mr. Leverage arrives. You don't need to wait on me—I'm used to taking care of myself."

"Everyone can do with a bit of pampering now and
then," she replied complacently. "And you look like
you need it more than most. You look worn to a
frazzle. While you're here I want you to take it easy.
Get out in the sun, go for long walks. All the land
around here is a protected wildlife area. Not that
you'll see wildlife any more threatening than rabbits
and maybe a fox or two, but it does make it nice and
secluded."

"I'd like that." Cassie averted her eyes from the
refrigerator door, suddenly remembering all too clearly the feel of it against her back as Bran pushed her up
against it.

"And I think I hear Mr. Leverage now. Why don't
you go on out. I'm sure you're anxious to see Meredith. Give her my love, and tell her I'll be stopping in
on my way home tonight."

It was with a sinking heart that Cassie walked out
into the warm spring morning to confront her erst-
while pilot—the very pilot who had made her swear
off airplanes for the rest of her life. "You would
have a Porsche," she said by way of a greeting, sighing. "I suppose you're going to drive the same way
you fly."

His scowl was less intense this morning, and for a

moment Cassie could see what had attracted Meredith to him. There was a solid air of strength and security about his sturdy frame, and his brown eyes, when they weren't glaring at her, would probably be warm and friendly. "That depends," he drawled, eyeing her across the car's shiny green hood.

"On what?"

"On how long you're going to stay."

Cassie hesitated, squinting across at him in the bright sunlight. "Two weeks," she replied. "Or until Meredith's well enough for me to leave." She tried a smile. "That'll give you plenty of chances to scare me to death."

With studied rudeness he climbed into the car, drumming his blunt fingers on the leather-covered steering wheel while Cassie followed suit. "I'll leave it up to you," he muttered. "You cause Meredith any more pain, and you'll wish you were never born."

Cassie looked at his set expression, sighed, and fastened her seat belt.

The next few days were reasonably comfortable. The unease of Gary Leverage's open hostility, the worry over Meredith's seemingly unchanged condition, and the fear that at any time Bran Rathburne would appear were balanced by the welcome and comfort of the house and Mrs. Bellingson. Cassie's days settled into a slothful pattern: sleeping late with breakfast in bed, followed by a visit to the pathetically pleased Meredith, then an afternoon of walking through the woods, reading, or working on a drastically altered résumé before eating dinner and retiring to the small sitting room with its stereo, comfortable couch, and the supply of brandy that went untouched. She had the uneasy feeling that all she had to do was drink too much again and Bran would reappear, either to take up where he had left off in the kitchen, or, even worse, not to.

Four days passed without a sign from him, but sometime during the night he came home. Cassie knew that much when she came upon Mrs. Bellingson making up Bran's bed one morning. The door was open, and with what she hoped passed for idle curiosity she strode in.

"Whose room is this?" she questioned innocently.

"Bran's," the housekeeper replied, pulling a pillowcase on to a king-size pillow. "Can't you tell?"

Cassie looked around her, impressed despite herself. The room was so very like him, she could understand Mrs. Bellingson's question. It was a man's room, no doubt about it, from the dark-hued Oriental carpets on the random-width floorboards to the plain maroon curtains at the windows and the king-size bed covered with a bear-claw patterned patchwork quilt. Never in her life had Cassie seen such a huge bed, but she presumed quite fairly that Bran needed it. After all, six feet four would have a hard time fitting in the standard double bed she was using.

At that unruly thought she swung around, banging her hand against the doorjamb and letting out a genteel curse. She had almost put him out of her mind, and then she had to make the mistake of wandering into his room. It would be awhile before she could get the image of that cozy-looking bed out of her mind.

"Did you hurt yourself, dearie?" Mrs. Bellingson inquired anxiously, smoothing the quilt over the bed before turning away to devote her full attention to Cassie.

"No, I'm fine. But why are you bothering with this room if he hasn't even been home in the last few days?" she questioned as her old bane, curiosity, came to the fore.

"And who says he hasn't been coming home at nights? His bed has been slept in, which, I may tell you, is a great relief. I hate the thought of that Barrow girl getting her claws into him."

"He's been sleeping at home?" Cassie echoed, some of her comfort vanishing.

"Every night."

"Well, I haven't heard a sound. He must come in very late. Perhaps he brings her with him. He could, for all I've noticed," Cassie suggested casually, wondering why the very thought would make her feel sick inside.

"No, he wouldn't do that," Mrs. Bellingson stated with great certainty. "Bran doesn't bring women here."

"Why not?"

Mrs. Bellingson led her out of the room, casting one last professional eye over the neat lines of the Early American furniture and the neatly made bed. "I don't exactly know." She shut the door behind them. "I might say out of respect for me and Meredith, but I don't think so. We're both broad-minded, and Bran does what he wants to do, no doubt about that. He has an apartment in the city, and I have little doubt he brings his lady friends there. After all, the man is hardly a monk. But he has yet to bring one home to spend the night. I suppose that's when I'll know he's serious about someone—when there are two for breakfast.''

It was Cassie's fifth night alone in the beautiful old house. She had adapted to the solitude in the evenings readily enough, enjoying the freedom and comfort of the place. She had taken to dressing for dinner, alternating between her cream silk suit and the slinky black silk dress she had bought on a whim and seldom worn. The black dress was normally just a bit too clinging and low-cut for her, albeit very elegant, but as she roamed about Bran Rathburne's house she enjoyed the feeling of its silky folds draping her body, which thankfully hadn't yet begun to exhibit the bulges she dreaded and knew full well were the consequences of Mrs. Bellingson's delicious, heavy food. The diamond earrings her mother had given her matched the sparkle in her eyes, and she floated down to the dining room to eat in solitary splendor, enjoying herself immensely.

The housekeeper had outdone herself that night with chicken cordon bleu, and as Cassie curled up on the blue couch with her stockinged feet tucked up underneath her, she smiled in lazy contentment. Meredith had finally agreed to her operation, her condition and mental acuity becoming more stable as the days passed. Gary Leverage had driven sedately enough each day, though Meredith steadfastly refused to see him. Things were improving steadily, and here Cassie sat in a beautiful room, Boz Skaggs playing on the stereo, a lovely meal in her stomach, and nothing to plague her. She had even succumbed to the temptation of a very small snifter of brandy, and as she held it to her lips her blood froze. Standing in the doorway, conjured up by an evil genie who knew the moment she reached for the decanter, stood Bran Rathburne.

"Good evening," she managed, resisting the impulse to jump to her feet and into the evening sandals beside the couch. She left her slim legs curled up beside her, eyeing him warily as she took another, deliberate sip of the brandy. The smooth warmth slid down into her stomach, providing her with a measure of courage she badly needed. This was the first time she'd seen him since that moment in the kitchen, and her cheeks flamed at the memory.

"Is there any of that left for me?" She had forgotten the low sensual drawl of his voice. "I remember you were making considerable inroads into it the first night you were here." He collapsed into a wing chair, his long legs stretched out in front of him, his face shadowed with exhaustion. He still had his coat on, but his tie had been long since discarded, and the white shirt was open halfway down his chest, exposing that remembered column of sun-bronzed flesh.

"Of course there is," she replied calmly enough. "I haven't had any since that night. But if you think I'm going to wait on you, you must be mad."

"I don't expect anything," he said in a quiet tone of voice, leaning back in the chair and closing his eyes. "I'm too tired to fight with you, Cassie. I've just spent all day at a very hostile board meeting, all evening at the hospital, making final arrangements for Meredith's surgery, and I'm beat.''

Cassie watched his weary face for a long silent moment. Deep lines had etched themselves in his narrow cheeks, his mouth was a thin gash, and his magnificent eyes were set in shadows. He had been pushing himself too hard, probably because he wanted to spend as little time as possible around her, she thought with a trace of guilt. On silent feet she rose from the sofa, poured him a brandy, and carried it to him. "Here," she said, placing it in one long-fingered hand. "You look like you need this."

His eyes flew open, meeting hers for a long pensive moment. The wariness was still there, combined with distrust and that indefinable something that still mystified her. "Thanks," he said shortly, taking a small, appreciative sip. His eyes slid over her body with its clinging black dress, and it was all Cassie could do not to cross her arms in front of her chest. The low-cut, clinging lines had precluded the use of a bra, and it felt as if Bran could see right through her thin covering. "Are you expecting someone?" he queried, his voice noticeably more hostile.

"No." She took the chance to move back to the sofa and the dubious protection a few yards would afford her. "I just felt like dressing for dinner. This house seems to appreciate small gestures like that."

He stared at her blankly. "I beg your pardon?"

A faint flush stained Cassie's pale cheeks. "I suppose you think that's idiotic of me, but for some reason I feel as if this house is a living thing. It responds to being treated well. It wants to welcome and comfort people. It..." She trailed off. "Now you'll be convinced I'm insane as well as an immoral gold digger."

"Not at all. I've often felt the same way. I'm merely surprised that you were sensitive enough to pick up on it." He took another sip of brandy. "You're not drinking your brandy." he observed.

Cassie, once faced with the intoxicating company of her reluctant host, didn't feel eager to continue with the heady brandy, but she obediently followed his lead and took another small, tentative sip. "I think I should find a hotel close to the hospital," she said abruptly.

Bran's winged eyebrows rose. "Why?" he questioned easily, some of the tension draining away from him.

Cassie hesitated, not wanting to exhibit more concern about his well-being than was strictly necessary. "Because you're obviously avoiding this house because of my presence. It won't do Meredith any good if you collapse from exhaustion, you know. If I stayed at a motel near the hospital, I could see her more often, and you could come and go—"

"No." The word was abrupt and unarguable.

Cassie silently counted to ten, then uttered the one word her irritation would allow her. "Why?"

Bran had closed his eyes again, but they flew open at her terse question. "For one thing," he began, his eyebrows arched mockingly over his weary eyes, "Meredith would be very upset if you weren't staying with me. She'd think I'd done something to offend you, and in her present weakened state all emotional upset should be avoided. Secondly, I am not avoiding the house because of your presence and drowning my sorrows in work. You aren't that important in my scheme of things. We're planning to move in new directions in the Foundation, and setting up the guidelines is a time-consuming, argumentative, damnable process, with everyone having his or her pet project and fighting to the death for it. I am weary of arguments at this point, so if you don't mind, we'll change the subject. I've made a few phone calls."

"That sounds ominous," Cassie murmured. "Checking on me? I doubt if you'll find anything particularly exciting."

Bran didn't bat an eye. "I had you checked out completely before I had you come down here," he said blandly. "And you're right—you've lived a singularly unexciting life. No, I made a few phone calls on your behalf to some prospective employers. There are several research projects at the university that might suit you. That is, I'm assuming you'd prefer to stay in the Princeton area."

Surprise kept Cassie silent for a moment. "Er... yes, if possible."

"We may as well start there. When you get back, call Henry Blythe at the Nutrition Department. He'll be expecting you. If you're interested in relocation, I have contacts in most of the eastern states and a few on the West Coast. Let me know."

Much as she hated to, necessity dictated that she thank him. "That's very kind of you," Cassie murmured reluctantly. "I appreciate your efforts."

His eyes met hers, latent amusement lighting their weary depths. "We made a bargain," he said briefly.

"It really kills you to be in my debt, doesn't it?"

"Yes." The answer came through gritted teeth.

"Good." He took another sip of brandy and turned toward the stereo. "I approve of your taste in music."

It was the first halfway positive thing he'd said about her, and the surprise of it left her speechless. Before she could recover he went on. "I also like that dress. Wear it tomorrow night." It was an order, not a request.

"Why should I?"

"Because I've been trapped into taking you to a dinner party at my stepmother's house. There'll only be about ten couples, so it shouldn't—"

"I have absolutely no intention of going out to dinner with you," she interrupted with calm self-assurance.

Bran swiveled around to give her the full force of his burning glare. "Do you think I didn't try to get out of it?" he demanded with his usual unflattering honesty. "It was scarcely my fault that dear Ellen chose that moment to pay one of her infrequent calls on Meredith. If I'd known she was there, I would have avoided her like the plague that she is."

"Why didn't you tell her we couldn't come? Why would she want me anyway? We haven't even met."

"That's exactly why she does want you. She's heard all about you. Didn't I warn you rumor travels fast in this area? She wants to see who finally ensnared me."

"Finally ensnared you?" Cassie echoed in an outraged shriek. "What kind of rumors are they?"

Bran's sardonic smile was hardly reassuring. "God only knows. Anything from a casual affair to a secret engagement, depending on who's talking. One thing is for certain, though. Everyone I know thinks we're intimately involved."

"Well, perhaps I should go with you. We can put a stop to that sort of nonsense before it goes any further—"

"That's where you're wrong, my dear," he interrupted, his eyes glittering in the lamplight. "We'll go for the express purpose of convincing them all that their speculations are correct."

"For heaven's sake, why?" She took another deep sip of her brandy, almost draining the glass in an attempt to control her agitation.

"Because that's what Meredith wants to believe!" he shot back. "Or hadn't you noticed? Hasn't she been asking you all sorts of—questions about how we're getting along, whether you like me, find me attractive?"

"Oh, no," Cassie said weakly. "She's been asking you the same sort of things about me?" At his terse nod she let out a muffled groan. "Surely you don't think it will help to encourage her in that fantasy? She's only doomed to disappointment eventually—unless you're planning to spend the rest of your life pretending to be enamored of me. Believe me, that will get awfully wearing."

"It already has!" he snapped. "Sooner or later she'll have to know the truth. It will be a simple enough matter to let our torrid affair die a natural death. By that time Meredith will be able to put up with having her wishes thwarted, and, if you cease your interference, she'll be back with Gary. He's the

best thing that ever happened to her, and with luck
she'll see that before long."

"What do you mean, interference from me? I
never said a word to her about Gary. I'd never even
met him until recently." Cassie was incensed.

The winged eyebrows rose disbelievingly. "But you
did warn her that men were shallow, selfish, and untrustworthy, didn't you? And that she shouldn't put
all her trust in one, because he'd only break her
heart?"

The sentiment was embarrassingly familiar. "Not
in so many words," she conceded. "I didn't say all
men were like that."

"But most of them. And you did warn her, didn't
you?"

"I didn't want her to be hurt!" she cried, then bit
her lip. She'd already said far too much to this sardonic man opposite her.

He stared at her for a long meditative moment, absently swirling the dregs of brandy in the Waterford
crystal snifter. "He really hurt you, didn't he?" he
asked suddenly, his voice low and compassionate, all
cynicism and contempt wiped from his face. But kindness was the last thing she could bear from him.

"Who are you talking about?" she demanded
hoarsely, determined to brazen it out.

"Whoever it was who ripped your heart out and tore
it into little shreds." There was still nothing but kindness in his slightly husky voice, a kindness that finally
undid her tenuous control. She had two choices—to get
mad or weep. She chose the former, rising to her full
height with regal rage.

"I fail to see that it's any of your concern." She fought back, setting the brandy snifter down on the coffee table with a snap. With unaccustomed clumsiness she knocked against the couch as she started a mad dash toward the door. Cassie got no farther than a few feet when Bran caught her, looming up before her, tall and strong and dangerous. The silver-blue eyes burned down into her angry, tear-filled ones, and the hands that caught her wrists were iron hard, tanned, beautifully sculptured, and so strong that her desperate struggles made no impression at all.

"You're always running away," he said meditatively, his voice low and beguiling. "Are you afraid of me, Cassie?" His words were soft and warm as a summer breeze, and she felt her resolve melting. Sternly she summoned it forth again.

"Of course I'm not afraid of you," she snapped, but her voice came out soft and low and intimate in response to his. "I'm simply tired and upset and I want to go to bed."

A small dangerous smile creased his mobile mouth. "That can be arranged," he whispered, moving his head closer.

Cassie's rage burst into full flower and her struggles began in earnest. "Not with you!" she gasped. "I don't even like you."

"That's quite all right," he murmured agreeably. "I don't like you, either." And his mouth caught hers midprotest, her mouth open to argue further.

Time seemed to stop, then lurch forward in slow motion. Dazed, Cassie felt his tongue invade the unresisting warmth of her mouth, the iron-hard hands pull her arms around his waist as he molded her pliant body against his taut lean length. She felt the edge of the sofa against her legs, and it was far easier to sink down beneath his weight than put up a fight she had no desire to win. Bran's mouth and his hands were seducing her, pressing her into the soft cushions, stroking her into a mindless, quivering submission. And her mouth and hands were answering, demanding a response from him that he wasn't lax in giving. As her tongue met his in a silent war of desire, her slender strong hands slipped beneath his open silk shirt to slide along his smoothly muscled flesh. The feel of the crisp hair on his chest intensified her longing, and mutely her hips arched to meet his as their mouths spoke in the only language in which they could communicate. Cassie was lost in a dream of desire and love, reveling in the pleasure Bran took in her body as his lips reluctantly abandoned hers and left a burning trail down her neck to the open front of her dress. Somehow the wrap front of the black material had been loosened, and with his hands and mouth he worshiped each round, perfect breast in turn.

"Cassie, Cassie," he murmured hoarsely against her petal-smooth skin. "Why do you have to be so damn beautiful? You're seducing me just as easily as you seduced Meredith." His mouth trailed back up toward her mouth as his hand reached along one exposed thigh. It wasn't until he reached her chin that he realized her body had become completely rigid with fury. Bran's hand stopped its enticing wanderings, and he raised himself off her body, looking down at her out of wary eyes.

Cassie took a deep breath to try to control the screaming rage that had effectively banished any trace of desire in her furious body. "Get your damn hands off me," she hissed. "How dare you?"

Bran made no move to lighten the weight of his strong frame pressing against her slender body. His face in the dim light was unreadable. "What's the problem?" he demanded in a cool, quiet voice. "Don't try to convince me this isn't what you want. We've known this was going to happen from the moment we met. Why deny it?"

"You conceited turkey!" She began struggling like a wild creature, thrashing and kicking with all her not-inconsiderable strength. With insulting ease he calmed her by the simple expedient of pressing down farther into the cushions, his hands catching her clawing ones and yanking them above her head. She had never felt more exposed and vulnerable in her entire life, and she knew full well by the intimacy of his body pressed against her that his desire ·hadn't lessened one bit.

"Are you going to calm down?" he inquired with deadly calm, taking in her flashing eyes and the stubborn set to her once-tremulous mouth. "I suppose you're angry because I said you seduced Meredith. I didn't mean in a physical sense. I know Meredith too well for that. But you seduced her emotionally and mentally, made her completely dependent on you—"

"Damn you, I did nothing!" Cassie cried, squirming beneath him.

"Of course you'd deny it," he said curtly, "just as you deny this...." His other hand caught her chin as he kissed her, hard and deeply and brutally. When he released her mouth, his breathing was as ragged as hers. "But it won't do any good. We both know where it's going to end, sooner or later." The fire in his eyes burned into hers. "In your bed, or mine. I'll leave the choice and the occasion up to you." With that he released her, getting to his feet in one swift movement, staring down at her as she lay, helpless and suddenly cold, alone on the sofa. "Just let me know." Without another word he turned and left the room.

With a small moan of shame and frustration Cassie curled up into a small ball on the sofa, hugging her arms around her to keep out the chill that had invaded her body when he left her. From far away she could hear the sound of his footsteps in the upstairs hall, the final slam of his bedroom door. She stared, unseeing, at the tiny-patterned flowers on the upholstery before she pulled herself to unsteady feet, thanking the stars that she had a lock on her door, that she hated Bran Rathburne, and that he had stopped in time. Giving herself to a man who hated her would have been the final blow to her crumbling self-respect, she knew. Tomorrow she would leave for Princeton. Meredith was doing well enough, and the surgery was scheduled for the day after tomorrow. Cassie would call her often, though she could ill afford the long-distance phone bills. But nothing, nothing in creation, was going to make her spend one more night under the same roof as Bran Rathburne, she decided.

Chapter Six

All Cassie's plans for an early exit were quickly swept away by the next morning, however. She slept soundly and dreamlessly, finally waking up after eleven with the strong spring sunlight streaming through the French doors. She sat out on the veranda, still in her ruffled cotton nightdress, drinking strong black coffee as she surveyed the lush greenery around her and the tangle her life was in.

Pride and common sense told her she should order a taxi, pack her bags, and leave this place and Bran Rathburne behind as fast as she could.

But...

There was Meredith, her life and body a crippled mess, counting on her. If she'd listen to anyone, she'd listen to Cassie. She had almost persuaded her to see Gary—bit by bit Meredith's misplaced resolve was weakening—and Cassie knew full well that fifteen minutes of uninterrupted time with Gary's honest love and concern would make Meredith see the light.

And there was her career. Bran had already made

the first steps toward helping her find a new job. If she left now, reneged on their agreement, she might as well not bother to call Henry Blythe at Princeton. If she did keep her side of the bargain, she knew with certainty that she could count on him, despite the fireworks between them.

And she had one more reason to stay: a very strong, real desire to humble the lordly Bran Rathburne, who set himself up as judge and jury, so sure he knew her. He'd condemned her without a hearing, and to add insult to injury, now seemed convinced that she was palpitating with desire for him.

Not that he wasn't worth desiring, she added fairly, pouring herself another cup of coffee and propping her bare feet up on the railing. As far as recklessly handsome, overbearingly self-assured man went, he just about topped the list. But that was the last sort of man she wanted. She would take great pleasure in showing him how unmoved she was by his considerable charms. Those long, long legs, the tanned clever hands that cupped her body so intimately, the dazzling silver-blue eyes that burned with desire when he looked down at her...

She set her coffee cup down hastily, spilling a bit. She was totally immune, she reminded herself. If she left today, he would see it as a sign of victory over her. And she wasn't going to let him win. Not a skirmish, not a battle, and definitely not the war!

Given her late start, it was just as well that her morning visit to Meredith had been canceled. A curious Mrs. Bellingson had informed Cassie that Bran would be picking her up at six that evening. They would stop by the hospital on their way out to dinner. Meredith had particularly requested it, so there was no way Cassie could reasonably object. "And he said to tell you that you should wear the black dress tonight," Mrs. Bellingson added, and immediately Cassie decided to go in jeans rather than wear that seductive dress in front of him again. "Not that it should matter, visiting her." The older woman sniffed disapprovingly.

"I shouldn't dress up to see Meredith?" Cassie teased.

"You know perfectly well it's not Meredith I'm talking about. It's that she-wolf their father married. I can't think what Bran's doing, exposing you to that pack of vultures. He does his best to steer clear of them, and I would think he'd do the same for you."

"What is so desperately awful about Ellen Rathburne?" Cassie queried, telling herself her curiosity was for Meredith's sake, not Bran's. Never Bran's. "Meredith never said much—just that Ellen hadn't been much of a mother, and that Bran didn't care for her."

Mrs. Bellingson snorted. "That's putting it mildly. There's a word for women like her—a word I wouldn't soil my lips with." She paused, turning from the pile of vegetables she was peeling. "And I certainly shouldn't tell you the depths of her wickedness. Not when you're going to have to accept her hospitality and be polite."

Cassie said nothing, waiting for the garrulous housekeeper to talk herself into it. "But, then," Mrs. Bellingson mused, dropping a paring knife, "it might be good for you to be forewarned. No sense going into the rattler's den without a weapon." She shook her graying head and sighed. "But, no, I shouldn't. My husband has always told me that gossip is my besetting sin. I try to temper it by only repeating the good things I hear about people, but with Ellen Rathburne I wouldn't be able to say a word." After wrestling with her conscience, she finally abandoned the struggle. "I'll leave it up to you. Do you want to know?"

A reluctant smile curved Cassie's face. "You wretch! You know perfectly well that I should say no. And you know perfectly well that I'm dying of curiosity. What did she do that was so awful?"

"Let me pour us a cup of coffee. I might even have half a cup of the real stuff myself. You've got to have real coffee with a good, cozy gossip."

A moment later they were both comfortably ensconced at the well-worn kitchen table, the vegetables momentarily forgotten, the coffee hot and rich in thick mugs. "The first Mrs. Rathburne," Mrs. Bellingson began with all the ceremony of an ancient storyteller seated by a camp fire, "died when the children were young. Bran had just turned fifteen, and little Meredith was ten. I think old Mr. Rathburne only took up with Ellen Barrow because he wanted another mother for his children. He couldn't have made a worse choice.

"Ellen Barrow was a divorcée of thirty when she married him—primarily for his money, of course. She hadn't gotten much of a settlement from her first husband. It was hushed up at the time, but eventually Bran discovered that the grounds had been adultery, on her side. Of course, that wasn't the way she told it."

Cassie's fertile imagination leaped ahead. "Well, what did she do? Cheat on the old man? I would think that would have been expected."

"Of course she did! With every man she could find. Mr. Rathburne either didn't know or didn't care. He was so caught up in his work, setting up the Foundation with his inheritance. He always felt guilty about all that money. Bran's the same way, just like his father. I don't know what it is they feel so guilty about. It isn't like Bran's grandfather was a robber baron or anything. He made their fortune through hard work and good investments. But that's neither here nor there.

"Bran's father took his first wife's death pretty hard, and he simply didn't have the interest to spare for his family anymore. He left Ellen to her own devices, and the children to Ellen. Everything went along well enough, until Bran turned sixteen."

"Oh, no," Cassie breathed, anticipating.

"Oh, yes." Mrs. Bellingson nodded grimly. "She began to notice her tall young stepson. He was a pretty boy back then, with a sweet and trusting nature. There's not much of that trust in evidence anymore, but I'm sure it's still there. She was always after him, looking for chances to touch him, showing him off to her friends. Then she started sneaking into his room at night, and there was nothing he could do. He couldn't go to his father and tell him his new wife was a lecherous trollop. Short of brute force he couldn't stop her from coming to his room."

"How awful!" Cassie found an unexpected rush of pity for the teenaged Bran, trapped between his stepmother's lust and his father's indifference. "What finally happened?"

"As you can imagine, he didn't want to leave Meredith to the old witch's clutches, or I'm sure he would have run away. Some of her male friends had already shown an interest in the girl, and Bran knew she was innocent enough to fall prey to those vultures. So he bided his time, until he was eighteen years old and got the first part of his legacy from his mother. And then he moved out, taking Meredith with him, and never went back."

"But he still sees Ellen? Socially, I mean? How could he?"

"He does, for Meredith's sake. Most everything he does outside the Foundation is for Meredith's sake. He fair dotes on her. Merrie's the only one he's ever loved since his mother died. She doesn't know about Ellen's nasty little habits, and pray she never finds out. Meredith doesn't understand things like that."

"They—Ellen and Bran, I mean—haven't renewed their affair since he moved out, have they?"

"Heavens, no. For one thing, Miss Ellen likes 'em young. She has a pretty boy in his early twenties dancing attendance on her right now. She never keeps them long. I don't know who tires of whom first— probably, it's mutual—but Bran wouldn't touch her with a ten-foot pole. He's her trustee, of course. Mr. Rathburne was too canny to leave her any money outright, and Bran keeps her spending under control as much as he can. He knows if she wastes her principal,

she'll come begging him for more, and that's the last
thing he wants. So he goes to dinner parties every now
and then, and everything is polite and civilized. But I
thought you ought to be warned, especially since..."
The words trailed off.

"Especially since...?" Cassie prompted.

"Her highness deigned to call me yesterday, trying
to find out everything she could about you. I'm afraid
you'll be coping with a jealous woman, Cassie."

"But I thought you said she likes her men younger
than Bran?"

"She does, indeed. But she still has a thing about
Bran. He's the only man who's always seen right
through her, and that drives her crazy. And any female who's enjoying his favor is in for trouble. Except
for Lucy, of course, Ellen's hand-picked successor. I
think Ellen feels that if Lucy manages to hook him,
she will have won in the long run."

"I am *not* enjoying Bran Rathburne's favor," Cassie said firmly, ignoring those passionate moments on
the blue couch. "If anything, I'm enjoying his disfa-
vor. If he had to choose between his stepmother and
me, I think he'd have a hard time deciding."

"That wasn't the impression I got. And I must say,
I know Bran a great deal better than you do," Mrs.
Bellingson observed slyly. "He may seem a bit gruff
at times, but his bark is far worse than his bite."

Cassie was to think back over that conversation as
she changed for dinner. She had been dreading the
dinner already. Her newfound knowledge of Ellen
Rathburne only solidified her reluctance. It was all she
could do to shake her sympathy for Bran. Such a trou-

bled adolescence would go a long way in explaining
his dislike and distrust of women, a dislike and distrust she had the feeling might extend beyond her.
And protecting Meredith had started way back, almost twenty years ago. It was no wonder he'd do anything for her, including consorting with an enemy
such as Cassie O'Neill.

Deliberately Cassie put the black silk dress in the
back of her closet and dressed in the pale silk suit.
Without a doubt the most expensive and elegant thing
she owned, it would give her a measure of confidence
among the Rathburnes' elevated society. The camisole top and straight skirt with its demure slit were
both quietly flattering and far more discreet than the
clinging black dress, and the jacket provided admirable protection from marauding eyes. Bran wasn't an
insensitive man. She doubted she would have to warn
him off. He would see the demure suit, recognize the
message in her polite, distant demeanor, and back
down. And pigs could fly, she thought.

Cassie surveyed her reflection one last time before
heading downstairs. She had heard the Jaguar pull up
more than a half hour ago, heard his long stride outside in the hallway as he hurried to his bedroom to
shower and change. He'd be ready soon, and the pale
lady in the mirror looked a far cry from the cool and
controlled female she wanted to appear. *I'm like a girl
on my first date,* Cassie thought dazedly as she put a
slightly unsteady hand up to smooth the stray wisps of
hair that had escaped her braids. The severe style did
little to contribute to the air of sophistication she
wanted to capture. Her troubled, defenseless honey-

brown eyes were shining out behind the thin lenses of her wire-rimmed glasses, her childishly freckled nose could only be described by that loathsome word *cute,* and her mouth, even with its coating of creamy lip gloss, betrayed her vulnerability every time.

"But you're not going to be vulnerable," she informed herself ruthlessly. "You're going to be brave and strong and independent, and not let that arrogant, overbearing man or his she-wolf of a stepmother get to you. Do you hear, Cassandra?" Cassandra nodded dubiously to herself. After throwing back her shoulders, she strode toward the door before nerves could overtake her.

She nearly ran straight into Bran, who was standing there, hand upraised, about to knock, and she caught herself just in time.

"What's the hurry?" he questioned lazily, his eyes drifting over her slender frame with that curious expression she was becoming used to. "You seem pretty eager for this evening."

"Hardly," she snapped back. "I thought I'd better hurry before I changed my mind."

"Changing your mind wouldn't have done you any good," he said, unruffled. "I wasn't about to allow you any choice in the matter."

"Just like you didn't allow me any choice in what I wear?" she taunted.

He cocked an inquiring eyebrow. "Well, Cassie, my angel, much as I prefer the black dress, I think you made the right decision. That suit is both charming and dignified. It will lend just the right touch to Ellen's crowd." He reached a tentative hand upward, brushing a loose strand of Cassie's chestnut hair with gentle fingers. "Do you always wear your hair that way?"

It was all Cassie could do not to slap his hand away. He was very handsome that night, dressed in a beautifully fitting black silk dinner jacket and tailored white pants that set off his long legs. His hair was still damp from the shower, and the black waves showed a surprising tendency to curl. The deep grooves down the sides of his cheeks had lessened in his unexpected good humor, the laugh lines around his beautiful eyes were creased, and his enticing mouth was actually curved in a gentle smile, with none of the former mocking quality that had set Cassie's nerves on edge.

She knew from experience that his charm was even more dangerous than his usual contempt. "Don't do that," she said quietly. "And I am not your angel." Anything to get that disturbing light out of his eyes, to have him move away from her. He was too damn close, she thought. The heat from his strong large body seemed to penetrate her light silk clothing, and the lovely smell of him, that seductive mixture of spicy after-shave, soap, and something indefinably male, was playing havoc with her senses. It was hard to remember how much he disliked her when he smiled at her so disturbingly.

Cassie's uneasiness had no effect on his surprising good temper. "For tonight you are," he replied equably, taking her arm in his strong, masterful grip. "And I expect you to play your part." A very faint note of grimness entered his voice.

"I'll play my part." She looked up at him, quite

fearlessly. "Despite what you believe, I keep my word."

A small cynical smile twisted his mouth. "When you look up at me out of those beautiful brown eyes, I could almost believe you," he said gently, "if I didn't already know just how untrustworthy you are." He gave her a forceful little yank, and Cassie had the strange conviction that he was as angry with himself as he was with her. "Remember to smile for Mrs. Bellingson."

Chapter Seven

Meredith's pathetic pleasure in their company did nothing to improve Cassie's combined bad temper and feeling of impending disaster. She knew as well as Meredith that the two of them made a striking couple, and it was all she could do not to cry out what a lie it was. The lie was too enticing to her, and it was far too tempting to try to believe it. Bran kept a strong, firm hand at the sensitive small of her back as he guided her through the hospital, the touch lightly possessive. But he didn't really want to possess her, she thought mournfully. At least, not for more than one night. And heaven only knew, she shouldn't want to be possessed.

"You look so nice together," Meredith breathed, sitting up amid the white hospital sheets and looking positively smug. "I think it's wonderful of Ellen to invite you."

"I wish you were coming, too, babe," Bran said lightly. "We'll be thinking of you all the time we're there."

"Well, I hope not!" Meredith managed a ghost of a

laugh. Her color had improved greatly, and she had finally gotten rid of the intravenous tube. "You two should be enjoying each others' company, getting to know each other."

Cassie felt a little nudge behind her, and obediently, she took her cue. "We already know each other quite well, Meredith," she said in dulcet tones, smiling shyly. Bran's arm came to rest lightly on her shoulder, and steeling herself, she looked up into the quizzical silver-blue eyes that smiled down at her tenderly.

That almost broke her resolve, and she felt her whole body stiffen. Before she could say anything, however, the hand that rested on her shoulder tightened warningly, and the look in Bran's eyes held a very definite threat.

"Are you feeling better about the surgery, Meredith?" Cassie queried, determined to change the subject. "I'm so relieved that you've finally agreed to it. The sooner your leg is properly set, the sooner you can get back to normal."

"You were the one who convinced me I had to do it, Cassie," she replied warmly. "I think I would have kept putting it off until it was too late if you hadn't come."

It was all Cassie could do not to flash a look of triumph at the tall man beside her. But, then, perhaps he wouldn't be pleased, she thought. He might see it as one more sign of her control—control she never wanted and had done her best to divest herself of. The hopelessness of it all threatened to overwhelm her, and with a determination and grace that effectively fooled Meredith's less than observant eyes, she shook off Bran's arm and moved a few feet away. "You would have come to your senses soon enough."

"Well, either way, we're both delighted that you're here," Bran said smoothly, and once more Cassie wanted to throw the lie back in his teeth. "In the meantime we better head for Ellen's. We're due there in fifteen minutes and we'll be late as it is." With equal grace he moved across the room and secured Cassie's reluctant hand in his, his fingers squeezing hers warningly. "We'll be in to see you tomorrow before the surgery, babe. And I don't want you to worry about it."

Cassie tugged uselessly at her imprisoned hand. "Would you rather I stay with you tonight, Meredith?" she inquired somewhat desperately. "If you're worried, you might feel better with company."

"Don't even think of it. They're going to give me something to help me sleep, and I wouldn't even know you're here, Cassie. No, you and Bran go and enjoy yourselves. That's what would make me happiest," she said wistfully. "The thought of you two out together, enjoying each others' company."

"But are you absolutely certain—"

"She's certain, Cassie," Bran interrupted with a spurious fondness, his eyes holding a hint of a glare beneath the indulgence. "Come along, angel."

Out of the corner of her eye Cassie saw Meredith preen at the endearment as Cassie was led with pseudo-tenderness out of the room. She could feel the tension in Bran's body as he hurried her through the spotless hallways and out into the May night air. It wasn't until he had her in the car that the storm broke.

"What the hell did you think you were doing in there?" he demanded roughly. "Meredith's no fool, you realize. A bit more of that and she might start thinking that everything isn't all hearts and flowers between us. I thought I warned you—"

"You've warned me, threatened me, coerced me!" Cassie shot back. "And I'm more than sick of it. I am not going to spend the evening smiling up at you and having everyone think we're lovers. I don't even want to spend another minute in your company. I want to go back to the house and retire with a good book. You can go on to your stepmother's. Tell them I'm sick, tell them I'm insane. I don't give a damn what you tell them, but I've had enough!"

Bran remained impassive throughout Cassie's outburst. "Are you finished?" he inquired evenly.

"Are you going to take me home?" she countered dangerously.

"No."

"Then I'm not finished. You can't make me—"

"I most certainly can." His voice was implacable. "Besides the fact that I'm a great deal bigger than you, you seem to forget I have a certain economic power over you. If you refuse to abide by the terms of our agreement, I'll simply have to force you. But you've spent the last week trying to convince me that you know the meaning of honor, that you live up to your obligations. Your obligations right now include accompanying me to my stepmother's house and putting a pleasant face on it. Are you going to go back on your word?"

His face was calm and expressionless in the dim

confines of the Jaguar as he waited patiently for her reply. Of course she had no option, she realized bitterly. Bran Rathburne was a past master at manipulating people to do his bidding. But somehow she would make him regret this latest piece of manipulation. He wasn't going to enjoy this evening if she could help it. He wasn't going to enjoy it one tiny bit, she decided.

"You don't leave me any choice," she said bitterly.

"No, I didn't think that I did." Without another word he started the car. As they sped along the deserted back roads Cassie allowed herself a furtive glance at his profile. At least he didn't gloat, but she would be damned if she'd let him get away with it. Her brain was working feverishly as the spring landscape whizzed by.

"I wouldn't if I were you." His voice interrupted her pleasantly sadistic reveries, and she jumped, startled.

"You wouldn't what?" Her voice was impossibly demure.

"Wouldn't do whatever it is you're thinking of doing. Revenge is an ill-advised activity. I know from experience. Why don't you accept defeat with good grace?" his slightly husky voice drawled casually.

"I don't accept defeat."

He cast a sudden, amused glance at her stony face. "No, I suppose not," he allowed. "Perhaps that's why you make such a fascinating adversary."

"Is that what we are?" She allowed her curiosity to overcome the animosity for a moment.

"I'd say so. *Enemy* is too harsh a term, *friend* is impossible. Of course, there are other possibilities, such as *employer, moral adviser*. Or *lover*." His voice was low and enticing, and Cassie felt her heart thud to a halt, then begin racing.

"That's what we'll be trying to convince everyone tonight, isn't it?" She made a strong effort not to let her agitation surface.

A small smile lit his face. "Oh, I don't think we have to go that far. As long as we remain reasonably civil everyone will be quite satisfied. I won't demand any more of you. Tonight." It was added almost as an afterthought, and a small shiver of anticipation ran through Cassie's veins. But then the thought of a perfect revenge blossomed forth, and she sighed with pure Machiavellian pleasure.

"I'm sure you'll be satisfied with my acting," she said sweetly, swallowing the evil laugh that threatened to erupt.

Once more he cast a glance in her direction, and there was a trace of worry in his eyes. "You'll behave yourself?" he demanded. "You'll keep your promise?"

"Oh, yes," Cassie breathed. "I'll behave myself."

The lights at Ellen Rathburne's perfectly restored plantation house blazed out into the spring evening as Cassie followed Bran's tall beautiful back up the wide front steps. "If you want people to think we're at least on speaking terms, I would suggest you wait for me," Cassie observed gently, sauntering up the steps with a leisurely pace she knew would goad him.

Bran came to an abrupt halt, his back still toward her as he waited for her to reach him. The tension in his body was palpable, and she smiled sweetly to herself. "If you're quite ready..." he grumbled.

Cassie laughed lightly, taking his arm. "More than ready."

"Is this your little friend, Bran darling?" A light, affected voice greeted them as they stepped inside the brightly lit hallway. "I've been on pins and needles, neglecting my other guests shamefully, just waiting to meet her. It's fortunate I have Lucy staying with me to take over some of my responsibilities." A vision floated toward them, a small slender perfect vision, from the tips of her tiny expensively shod feet to her beautiful coiffed rich black hair, which didn't have a trace of gray in it, framing a face as characterless and smooth as an adolescent's. Only the eyes held any expression, and that was avid hostility at variance with the smile on her red-painted lips.

"Cassie, this is Ellen Rathburne." Bran made the introductions in a bored tone of voice. "Cassie O'Neill."

Ellen held out a smooth manicured hand, the long red fingernails looking like claws. "I'm delighted to meet you, my dear Cassie. I had no idea you were such a taking little thing. And I love your glasses—they give you such an enchantingly forbidding look. You must call me Ellen." The mouth continued to smile, exposing perfect teeth. The hand that Cassie shook was soft, limp, and cold.

Cassie tightened her grip, pumping enthusiastically and beaming at her hostess's wince of pain. "Gosh, I'm so glad to meet you, Ellen!" she said, her voice loud and cheerful and slightly nasal. "I've always wanted to meet Bran's mother. Why, you look just like him. I always think it's so far-out to see the way people resemble each other. And it's nice you're still so close. Most men I know practically disown their mothers when they get past sixty. But then, I shouldn't be surprised at how sweet Bran is. I know only too well what an absolute doll he can be. Don't I, Bran darling?'' She turned and batted her eyes up into Bran's astonished face, wishing she had some chewing gum to add to the effect.

"I am hardly Bran's mother,'' Ellen said in icy tones, the smile fading but still valiantly clinging to her lips. "I married his father when I was merely a child and Bran a young man. There's always been a special bond between us, hasn't there, Bran?'' she cooed up at him.

Taking up the gauntlet her hostess had thrown down, Cassie threaded her arm through Ellen's confidingly, dragging the slight figure along with her as she charged toward the sound of voices and laughter. "How sweet. And I'm so glad you like my glasses, Ellen,'' she bubbled. "I lost my contact lenses last night. It was all Bran's fault, and so I told him, but he would insist on having a wrestling match, of all things. And that rug by his bed has such a deep pile. Mind you, I love it. It feels great when you're barefoot, but it's no good at all for finding contacts.''

"I know the rug well,'' Ellen said thinly. "I helped him choose it.''

"Well, you see!'' Cassie said admiringly. "I guess he couldn't have a better mother—I beg pardon, step-mother. Listen, if you really like that rug, you can have it when we redecorate. It wouldn't really go with the color scheme I had in mind. I thought I'd get a crushed red velour bedspread and maybe wall-to-wall carpeting, spruce the place up a bit. You know the sort of thing I have in mind."

"I'm afraid I don't." Her hostess's voice was faint. "I don't quite understand, Bran." She turned her head to her stepson beseechingly as she fought against Cassie's determined grip. "I hadn't realized there was any sort of understanding between the two of you. After all, you scarcely know each other. Surely you're not going to rush into anything rash?"

Before Bran could say anything Cassie jumped in. "Well, we're not saying anything officially, of course. But it happens like that sometimes." After releasing Ellen's arm, she snapped her fingers under her nose. "Bam—just like that. Bran and I knew we were soul mates the moment we met. Didn't we, sweet-ums?" She steeled herself to face him, wondering how long she'd have to wait before he exploded and hurried her out of the house.

To her amazement he was smiling down at her, the perfect image of the besotted suitor. "We certainly did, Cassie darling," he murmured, his eyes promising retribution. "Can I get you both a drink?"

"Just a beer, sweet-ums," she replied, her eyes an angry challenge. "And you don't need to bother with the glass—I'll drink it from the bottle. Tastes better that way," she confided to her horrified hostess.

"I—I'm not sure if we have any beer," she said faintly. "You might check with Willis, Bran dear. And I'll have vodka on the rocks. A double," she added

with feeling. "Come in"—her voice quavered, then
strengthened—"come in and meet my other guests,
Cassie. I'm sure they'll be absolutely fascinated."

"Far out. I love to meet new people. Is my outfit all
right?" she added with just the right touch of anxiety.

Ellen was taken aback. "Why, it's perfectly lovely,
my dear."

Cassie sighed gustily. "Well, I'm glad of that. Bran
bought it for me. I thought it was pretty plain, myself.
I was all set to wear the prettiest little dress. Flame-
colored silky sort of stuff, with the neckline down to
here and slit up the thigh." She made appropriate gestures that had Ellen on the verge of passing out. "But
Bran said he'd be too jealous of all the other men if I
wore anything so sexy, so I did as he told me. He likes
to be overbearing, doesn't he?"

"I really wouldn't know," her hostess said faintly,
leading Cassie into a living room filled with beautifully dressed, perfectly turned-out people who were
doing their best not to stare at the noisy interloper in
the elegant silk suit. Grimly Ellen began the introductions, halting long enough for Bran to present them
with their drinks. He handed Cassie her bottle of Hei-
neken beer with a light of reluctant amusement in his
eyes.

"I hope this will do," he said gently.

Cassie shrugged. "Well, I prefer American beer—
Bud or Schlitz—but I guess this'll have to do. You
can't be choosy when you go out, can you?" she said
philosophically. After taking Ellen's reluctant arm
once more, she gave her an enthusiastic squeeze that
came close to cracking several bones. "Don't you

worry your head about it, Ellen. I'm sure you're great at party-giving. You just couldn't think of everything.''

"I appreciate your forbearance, my dear," Ellen said dryly, and Cassie could see her trying to catch Bran's eye to give him a speaking glance. Bran, however, wasn't the slightest bit interested in sharing secret thoughts with his stepmother, and Cassie felt his arm slide gently around her waist, the fingers biting into her soft flesh.

"Don't worry about Cassie and me, Ellen," he said smoothly. "I'll make sure she meets people."

"Oh, but—" Cassie started to argue, and the fingers bit in deeper, causing her to gasp involuntarily.

"Are you all right, Cassie?" The startled reaction hadn't escaped Ellen's unfriendly eyes.

With a low bawdy chuckle Cassie turned and swatted Bran on the shoulder. "Naughty boy!" she simpered. "You shouldn't do things like that in public. What will your stepmother think of you?" She heard Ellen's indrawn hiss of horrified breath, but her attention was all for her companion.

The expression on Bran's dark handsome face was unreadable. His sensuous mouth was curved in an obligatory indulgent smile, his nostrils were flared in anger, and his silver-blue eyes had taken on an arctic hue that was at the same time quite steamy. She wished more than anything that she could put a name to that look, but it was beyond her. Whether it was contempt, hatred, dislike, or just possibly something more positive, she couldn't quite tell. Perhaps a bit of everything, all wrapped up in a hostile package. And yet, he seemed more amused than angry at her antics tonight, and she decided to up the ante.

Waltzing closer, she raised her lips to his ear, being deliberately provocative. She knew from the hushed atmosphere that despite their rigid code of behavior, most of Ellen's guests were staring at the tableau in disbelieving fascination.

"You should behave yourself, sweet-ums," she cooed, placing her lips just below his ear. She could feel the pulse pounding beneath her mouth, and she took advantage of the audience to press her slender body against his taut lean strength. "We had better be on our best behavior, hmmm?" Her voice was loud enough to carry as she reached up on her tiptoes and nipped lightly at his ear. She could feel a shudder run through his body, and with deceptive care he reached out and caught her hand, moving her carefully away, his fingers biting painfully into her wrist.

"We'd both better behave ourselves, Cassandra," he warned, a hoarse note beneath his deliberately light tone.

By this time Cassie had had enough of his abuse. "I agree completely, sweet-ums," she said soulfully, raising his wrist to her mouth to deposit a lingering kiss there for the delectation of the onlookers. What they failed to realize, however, was that as her lips closed over his warm flesh her teeth sank in, and she bit him as hard as she possibly could, hoping to draw blood.

To her dismay he neither flinched nor pulled away, but merely stood staring down at her impassively as she did her best to hurt him. She felt trapped by her own foolishness and sickened by her need to hurt him, yet she could think of no way she could gracefully release his wrist. It was with real gratitude that she heard a new voice, one curiously akin to Ellen's' lightly affected tones, drawl in her ear.

"Well, Bran. I wasn't sure you'd be able to make it after all," the woman said, and with the sudden buzz of conversation Cassie was able to release Bran's wrist. Before she could move away, however, his abused hand reached back and caught hers, in a light but firm grip with none of the bruising intensity, and his expression was still noncommittal.

"Lucy." He acknowledged the newcomer. "I don't believe you've met Cassie."

The blond porcelain doll smiled, it seemed, with a hundred large white teeth. "I don't believe I have. However, the kitchen was absolutely abuzz, and your fame has spread all the way out to the patio. It's small wonder we've seen so little of Bran when he has such an entertaining companion." Lucy tried for an arch look of commiseration with the man beside her, but Bran ignored her overtures as he had Ellen's.

"Little wonder, indeed, Lucy," he murmured, pulling Cassie's unresisting body closer to his warmth. "Cassie and I have been very busy."

The little doll didn't look any more pleased than her aunt, but she managed to put a better face on it. "Well, I'm glad you've found someone, darling," she drawled. "But in the meantime, I gather dinner is ready. I believe Cassie is sitting with Governor

Winkley, and you, lucky man, are my dinner partner.''

Instinctively Cassie tightened her grip, causing Bran
to look down at her with mingled surprise and amusement. "Cassie will enjoy that," he said smoothly.
"She does love to meet people, don't you, darling?"

There was nothing she could do but release his arm
and smile brightly. She was being tossed to the
wolves, and there was nothing she could do to save
herself, except brazen it out and pretend she didn't
mind as the lovely blonde caught Bran's relinquished
arm in a clinging grip. Governor Winkley stepped forward with all the aplomb of one accustomed to asso-
ciating with the lower orders, and Cassie watched
Bran and Lucy lead the way to the dining room with
mournful eyes, ignoring the retired politician's smooth
platitudes as her ears strained for the conversation
ahead of her.

"Honestly, Bran, how could you!" Lucy was hiss-
ing, amusement and outrage etched delightfully on
her perfect features. "Ellen almost had a stroke."

"I don't know what you're talking about, Lucy."
Bran's voice was unruffled.

"Don't you?" She was plainly skeptical. "Well, I
won't say another word, I promise, but I can't understand— Good heavens, what happened to your wrist?
You're bleeding."

At that tactless outcry Cassie nearly burst into tears.
Bran's muffled reply made it no easier on her. "Just a
scratch, Lucy. There's a piece of loose trim on the
Jaguar. Please don't fuss."

"But—"

"Enough," he ordered, his usually imperious,

overbearing self, Cassie noted. And Lucy, just like all the other women she had observed in Bran's life, immediately kowtowed. Cassie couldn't help but wonder if she had any fight left in her, either.

"Shall we get you another beer?" the ex-governor inquired tactfully as he seated her miles away from her adversary.

Heaving a gusty sign, Cassie nodded. "Far out," she replied in sweet tones. "Make sure it's in the bottle, though, Guv."

Chapter Eight

Ellen and Lucy did their effective best to keep Bran safely out of reach of Cassie's clinging arms. She had to make do with elaborate winks, blown kisses, leers, and sighs. Bran watched her from across the room, his attention fixed fully on her and not on his stepmother or his girl friend. His eyes were unreadable in that light, and Cassie was just as glad. Her imagination was running out at this rate, and he wasn't even near enough to appreciate the consummate vulgarity of her performance.

When the dancing started, Cassie viewed the situation with fresh promise. Before she could make her move, however, Ellen intervened, making doubly certain the two of them had no chance to make it to each others' arms. A steady throng of elderly businessmen were presented for Cassie's delectation, and she had to suffer through pinching, squeezing, foot-treading, heavy breathing, and all the other myriad torments her behavior incited. Her only consolation was to see Bran similarly punished, going from one elderly matron to another, his expression always perfectly polite and interested as his eyes would seek her out, the heat of his gaze warming her bones.

She was on her second dance with the surprisingly graceful Governor Winkley when Bran finally cut in. "I hope you don't mind, Governor." Bran's voice was cool and polite, and reluctantly the elderly politician relinquished his partner.

"I don't know if I ought to, Rathburne. She's pretty light on her feet, this one is. I don't blame you for being so enamored." After giving her one last confiding wink, he ambled off, and Cassie looked up into Bran's unreadable face before stepping into the circle of his arms.

He pulled her very close, his hands firm but not rough as he pressed her head against his unyielding shoulder. For a moment she closed her eyes in sudden relief as she stumbled against him, feeling curiously like a weary traveler who had finally found her way home. She could feel his heartbeat beneath her cheek, feel the steady measure of his breathing, which matched hers. For a moment she stumbled against him in sudden self-consciousness, but his hand behind her back supported her.

They danced in silence for a while, their bodies curiously in tune, and Cassie followed his lead with mindless instinct as her body reveled in the feel of his leanly muscled length.

"I'm sorry," she whispered suddenly.

He smiled down at her. "Sorry for what?"

"For biting your wrist. I didn't mean to hurt you," she muttered against the fine weave of his jacket.

"Didn't you? I rather thought you had. Not that I didn't deserve it."

She looked up in surprise, then. "Close your mouth, Cassie," he admonished, "you'll catch flies. Which doesn't mean," he continued, "that I'll let you get away with that again. You try something like that once more, and I'll turn you over my knee and spank you. And if you don't think I mean it, you should ask Lucy. I've been known to spank women for irritating me."

"You—you—" Words failed her as she glared up at him, all softness vanishing in the light of this recent threat.

"Sadist?" he suggested cheerfully.

"You're sick!" she hissed.

"There's nothing sick in wanting to sock someone you feel richly deserves it. Witness my bloody wrist," he countered.

"I don't have to listen to this," she stormed, starting to pull away. She got exactly nowhere. His hands were iron encased in velvet, and she could move no more than a few inches in his seemingly tender grasp. Ellen's guests were now viewing them with tolerant affection. The sight of two young people supposedly in love managed to harden even their judgmental hearts. And Cassie knew with sudden despair that all her struggles would simply look as if she were squirming closer to Bran.

"I'd hold still if I were you, Cassie," he murmured, his hot breath caressing her ear. "You're exciting me with all that wiggling." To prove his point he pressed his hips insinuatingly against hers, and she let out a little choke of outrage.

"Now I *know* you're sick!" she gasped. "I'll get even with you for this, Bran Rathburne, I swear I will. If it's the last thing I do."

"But that's what you've been trying to do all evening, isn't it? And it hasn't worked very well. You've provided me with admirable protection from two women who were far too possessive, given Landover society something to talk about for weeks to come, and given me considerable amusement. Where did you learn this little act from, anyway? It's very well done."

"You may be amused," she said icily, "but be assured I've only begun. By the time I'm finished with you, you'll be—you'll be—"

"Begging for mercy? Or forgiveness?" he mocked. "Don't count on it. Whatever you can dish out I can meet and double. You may as well surrender."

The sexual connotation was as clear as the feel of his desire against her silk-clothed skin. "Never!" she shot back.

A smile lit his face. "We'll see. In the meantime, I don't think I'd better press my luck. We'll leave when this dance is over."

"And what if I don't care to leave?"

"Then I'll put you over my shoulder and carry you out. Don't think I can't do it. I'm a hell of a lot bigger than you and I've hefted larger bundles." His fingers tightened warningly on her hand. "Are you going to go peacefully?"

Cassie considered her options. At this point it looked as if she'd get off lightly for her behavior. If she were wise, she'd let things go, but then, she'd never been known for her prudence. And she couldn't let him think he'd gotten the last word. Not a skirmish, not a battle, she had promised herself.

"I'll go," she murmured. "I don't know about peacefully."

As Bran led her across the room to make their farewells to their less than delighted hostess, Cassie racked her brain for something effective to seal the evening. A fight, she thought, with her slapping him across the face and storming from the house? No, she'd inflicted enough violence upon him for one night, she decided. She had strong doubts that she'd get away with any more physical abuse, no matter how richly he deserved it.

Could she be drunk? she asked herself. Stagger into tables and giggle noisily and tipsily, clinging to Bran, barely able to support herself? But too many people had watched with horror as she slugged beer from the bottle, and there was no way she could convince people she was sloshed on two bottles of beer, she knew.

"Leaving so soon?" Ellen said silkily, pouting her perfect lips. "I've so enjoyed meeting you, Cassie dear. You must come back and visit me often," she said with perfect insincerity.

"Why, thanks, Ellen. I'd love that. Maybe we could get together for some girl talk. I'd love to hear all about Bran when he was a little boy, and what better person than someone who watched him grow up?" she bubbled, enveloping the reluctant Ellen in a crushing embrace. "And I'm sorry we have to leave so soon, too. I was just beginning to enjoy myself, but

Bran here insisted on getting me back so's he could have me all to himself. Didn't you, sweet-ums?'' She glanced upward and watched his handsome features slip into a brief scowl before his company mask was in place again.

"Yes, thank you for a lovely evening, Ellen," he began smoothly, sounding, Cassie thought, like something out of an old Cary Grant movie. And then inspiration struck. If Irene Dunne could do it, so could she.

"My purse!" she shrieked. "Where's my purse? Don't anybody move!"

Ellen stared at her, dumbstruck. Before she could utter the faint protest that was forming on her carmine lips, however, Bran took chargé.

With brute force he yanked Cassie from the room, so that she was flying after him out the hallway and down the front steps, barely able to keep her balance. By the time they reached the car they were both panting from exertion and fury. After yanking open the door for her, he finally released her arm. "Get in," he ordered.

"But my purse—" she began innocently.

"Can it, Cassie! I saw that movie, too. Are you going to get in, or am I going to stuff you in?" The idea obviously pleased him, and with more haste than dignity Cassie scrambled into the front seat of the Jaguar. The hurried ride back to Bran's house was accomplished in furious silence. The moment he screeched up to the front door she was out of the car and racing across the gravel driveway, determined to reach the relative safety of her bedroom. The look on his face in the darkened car had bordered on brutal, and Cassie decided the better part of valor was to get as far away as she could, as fast as she could.

Bran caught up with her in the dark hallway. She was on the third step toward the second floor when his arm shot out and caught her, spinning her around to face him with all the force in his strong body. Her ankle turned on the stairs, and she fell into his arms. But there was nothing welcoming about them this time. Pushing her up against the wall, he placed his hands on either side of her head, imprisoning her effectively.

"Get your hands off me," she spat furiously, rage, fear, and something else warring for control.

But his rage obviously matched her own—even outdistanced it. "I'm not touching you," he replied, and with a shock Cassie realized it was true. The heat from his body seemed a tangible thing, but actually he was pinning her like a struggling butterfly with the sheer force of his personality.

"Then let me go," she whispered. The only light that lit the cavernous darkness was a small lamp in the upstairs hallway, casting ominous shadows around them. The light and dark increased the impression of brutality in Bran's face. "Please."

His eyes glittered with anger, contempt, and that other emotion, which Cassie was finally able to recognize. It was desire, and the thought both warmed and frightened her. "Please?" he echoed mockingly. "I thought you were unacquainted with manners after tonight. After such a delicious performance, you almost had me convinced."

"Bran?" she pleaded throatily, not knowing what she was pleading for. He was so close, so damn close. He could easily hurt her, and yet she knew he wouldn't.

He stared at her for a long moment. "Damn you, Cassie," he said succinctly. And then his mouth descended, pinning her against the wall, as his tongue angrily invaded the warm sweet interior of her mouth.

Cassie was helpless before the onslaught as he held her immobile with his body, his mouth hard and punishing on her soft lips. There was nothing she could do but stand and endure it, fighting the impulse to slide her arms up and around his neck. And then she fought it no longer, running her hands over his chest, pressing her slender body against his, meeting his mouth fully, the tip of her tongue reaching out shyly to touch his marauding one.

Suddenly the embrace changed. It was no longer a punishment as Bran's arms slid around her, cupping her sweetly and gently against his body. His mouth left hers and trailed a fiery path down her neck in short, hurried kisses that left her breathless and aching for more. She could feel the heat of his desire against her, and an answering fire glowed from deep within her body. For a moment she forgot everything — his contempt, his hatred, her fury with his overbearing tactics. All that remained was his body pressing hungrily against hers, his mouth moving back to claim hers once more as she sank willingly into a morass of desire that threatened to overwhelm her. His hands slid under the camisole top she was wearing, and one large warm hand cupped her breast, his thumb rubbing tenderly against the nipple confined in a thin wisp of a bra. A moment later he dispensed with the front clasp, and it was flesh on flesh. His warm, slightly callused fingers held and caressed the creamy smooth skin of her brest and its straining nipple.

"Are you still going to fight it, Cassie?" he whispered in her ear, his tongue tracing delicious designs on the sensitive skin. "Or are you going to admit that you want me as much as I want you?"

Only distantly did she hear that taunting voice. Her hands slid up his chest, to meet with the frustrating obstacle of his shirt. Desperately she struggled with the hidden buttons on the formal shirtfront, needing the feel of his broad hair-roughened chest against her hands, her skin. More than anything she wanted to erase all thought and doubt, to drown in the tidal wave of feeling that was sweeping over her at the behest of his hands and mouth, but his buttons proved impossibly stubborn—just stubborn enough to make her realize what she was doing.

"No!" She yanked herself out of his arms with a sudden, completely unexpected jerk, and he fell backward against the railing. He stayed there, staring at her out of fathomless eyes.

"You do like to tease, don't you?" he said quietly, his voice like a whiplash. "Hot and cold all the time. Why don't you make up your mind?"

"I have made up my mind," she shot back, trying to control her heavy breathing and the telltale pounding of her heart beneath the thin camisole. "Yes, I want you, Bran Rathburne. And yes, I'm going to fight it. I place too high a value on my self-respect to give in to someone who thinks I'm a—a—"

"How do you know what I think you are?" he questioned softly, his uneven breathing betraying the deliberately blank expression in his eyes.

"You've made it more than clear."

He took a step away from her, hesitated a moment, then sighed. "I should tell you that I've decided you didn't mean any real harm, either with Meredith or with the Nutri-Center. I think, for whatever reason, that your sense of morality is a bit...elastic."

"Thank you so much." she hissed. "Well, let me tell you this. It's not elastic enough to include going to bed with a man who hates me, all for the sake of pure animal lust. It'll never happen, Bran."

"Never is a long time, Cassie," he said softly.

"Not long enough." And not caring if it looked like the retreat it was, she turned and ran the rest of the way up the stairs, not stopping until she was safe in the haven of her bedroom.

Chapter Nine

It had been an exhausting day, Cassie thought as she
shoved a weary hand through the wisps of hair that
had escaped her coronet of braids. The sleepless
night had set the pace for it, followed by Bran banging on her door at the ungodly hour of six thirty, a
mere two hours after she'd finally dozed off. He informed her that if she wished to be at the hospital to
await the outcome of Meredith's surgery, she would
have to be ready in a half hour. The operation was
scheduled for eight o'clock, his voice announced
coolly, and he would be damned if he would miss the
chance to see her before she went in due to Cassie's
lazing about.

It was obvious to Cassie that Bran hadn't slept well,
either. There were shadows beneath his eyes, and the
grooves in his tanned lean cheeks were more deeply
etched. The trip to the hospital was made with white-
knuckled speed in complete silence, and all for nothing, as Meredith was already under sedation when
they arrived.

The next four hours were without question the most

uncomfortable ones Cassie had ever lived through. With a glowering, silent Bran on one side, a depressed, impossibly negative Gary Leverage on the other, and neither gentlemen deigning to address a word to her, Cassie wondered how long she could survive without jumping out a window. The fumbling ministrations of the hospital volunteer to treat them as a united family only exacerbated the situation, and it was all Cassie could do to keep herself from flinging her arms around the doctor's neck in tearful gratitude when he came to report that Meredith had made it through the operation with flying colors. As it was, she contented herself with a watery smile that faded swiftly as she watched her reluctant companions disappear without a word. Gary stalked out, his face shuttered with relief and pain, and Bran, turning his broad back to her, strode off in earnest conversation with the surgeon, not sparing even a tiny glance back at Cassie's forlorn figure.

"Can I get you another cup of coffee, dearie?" the volunteer inquired anxiously, offering the only comfort she was allowed to dispense. Having already partaken of close to five cups, Cassie shook her head. With great calm she strode out of the waiting room, out of the hospital, and into the parking lot. To her relief Bran, in his abstraction, had forgotten to lock the car. After sliding behind the steering wheel of the silver Jaguar, she leaned her head down on the leather-covered wheel and shook with racking sobs.

She passed Bran on her way back into the hospital an hour later, her head held high, her eyes only slightly red-rimmed. The look he cast her was cursory, his thoughts obviously elsewhere. "I'll be back to get you around six," he said abruptly.

"There's no need. I can just as easily get a taxi. As a matter of fact, since Meredith's come through the surgery so well, there's no real reason for me to stay on in Virginia, is there? I could go back and pack and catch a train—"

"No!" This time she had his full attention, and his silver-blue eyes glared down into hers, making her feel like a trapped rabbit. "You gave me your word you'd stay two weeks. It's less than a week, Cassie. I thought you assured me I could trust you." His voice was silken, but there was no mistaking the challenge in his light tone.

"You can trust me. I just thought, since Meredith's going to be all right, that—"

"You thought wrong," he interrupted implacably. "If you expect my help in salvaging the shambles of your career, then I suggest you keep your word. I'll be back at six. Unless, of course, you'd rather go back to the farmhouse right now."

"No, thank you." Her voice was a study in politeness. "I'd like to spend some time with Meredith." Her career, she thought belatedly. How long had it been since she'd given it first priority? She'd spent far too much time concentrating on Bran Rathburne's debatable merits and not enough on her very shaky future. Bran's cool nod of dismissal had done little to warm her cold thoughts, and Meredith's drugged, dreamy state offered no distraction. The hours crept by, leaving Cassie with only her own disturbing company.

She was a fool to count solely on Bran to get her out of the mess her career was in, she realized. She could call Eliza that night to see if she had found out anything concerning Dr. Alleyn's falsified data. She thought about writing to the board of directors, demanding a full investigation and a hearing. Surely if she made enough of a fuss, the truth would eventually come out. Alleyn couldn't have covered his tracks that effectively, could he? she thought. Did she dare take the risk? At this point they'd hushed up the scandal. She could still find work, perhaps in some other part of the country. If she actually went so far as to raise a stink, level counteraccusations against the respected Dr. Stanley Alleyn, then she would be risking everything. As she stared at Meredith's pale, drawn countenance she tossed the idea back and forth in her mind, coming no closer to an answer as the hours passed.

It was a hot, sticky day, more like July than early May. Cassie's loose cotton shirt stuck to her skin, her braids felt like leaden weights on her head, and her spirits flagged still further beneath the oppressiveness of the weather. The arrival of Lucy Barrow, smack on the stroke of six, did little to improve her mood, especially when she learned the reason for her visit.

"Hi, there!" Lucy's cool blue eyes surveyed her with elegant disdain. "Bran asked me to give you a ride home. I wanted to see how Meredith was doing, anyway, and rather than have him make an extra trip out to the farm before meeting me for dinner, I thought I could save him the trouble. How is she?"

She cast a cursory, disinterested glance over Meredith's sleeping figure.

"She's resting," Cassie muttered unnecessarily. "I told Bran earlier that I could get a taxi."

"But he doesn't seem to quite trust you, does he?" Lucy said sweetly, a mocking smile on her pretty mouth. "I wonder why?"

"Why don't you ask him?" countered Cassie, her rage simmering just beneath the surface. That he would dare, would dare to discuss her with this predatory female! And after the way he had kissed her last night, she thought. But, of course, there were no sweet words, no promises accompanying those kisses. All his sweet words were saved for the pretty, useless creature beside her, Cassie told herself firmly as she followed Lucy's slender figure out to her small imported car. It was a sleek Mercedes, Cassie realized with a sinking heart. Didn't anyone besides her have an aging VW?

It took all Cassie's wits to fend off Lucy's none too subtle attempts to plumb the depths of Bran and Cassie's relationship. She seemed to take Cassie's more subdued behavior in her stride, but what started out amusing Cassie soon ended as supremely irritating, so that when she climbed out of the car in front of the deserted farmhouse, it was all she could do not to slam the door in Lucy's smug certainty.

"Needless to say, don't expect Bran back tonight," the woman cooed. "He usually spends the night, and I haven't seen anything since you've arrived that would lead me to think he'd change his ways. Sleep well, Cassie dear. Such a pleasure to have met you."

She took off with a little spurt of gravel, and the darkening sky grumbled with an anger that matched Cassie's mood.

"Don't bother to expect Bran back, Cassie dear," she mocked in a cloying little tone. "I'll Cassie dear you," she threatened to the disappearing automobile.

But the anger soon faded, leaving her exhausted and depressed. Mrs. Bellingson had already left, and the house seemed curiously empty as Cassie wandered about disconsolately. In solitary splendor she ate an ice-cold salad and drank some iced tea, and afterward she roamed through the house. Even Eliza was out to her phone call, making Cassie feel more alone and abandoned in the hot night air. There were no sad movies on television, and the thought of brandy made her ill.

Finally, at a few minutes past nine o'clock, she went up to bed. A cool shower went a long way toward helping her state of mind. Her thin cotton nightgown was deliciously cool, and with her wet curtain of hair down her back she climbed into bed and began the first draft of her letter to the board of trustees of the Thompson Nutri-Center. There were some things in this life that were beyond her control, she knew, but she was damned if she was going to take the coward's way out with her career. She was well on her way to disaster, and it was better to end with a bang than a whimper. There was the faintest hint of a breeze from the veranda, wafting through the open French doors. The thunder still rumbled ominously in the background, and Cassie uttered a small, futile wish that the storm would hold off until the daylight hours. The

house already felt too large and empty—a violent
storm would only intensify the effect.

Tomorrow, she thought dreamily, putting the finished draft to one side, tomorrow she would go home,
and to hell with Bran Rathburne. She didn't need him
to salvage the remnants of her career. She had done
nothing wrong, and she wasn't going to spend another
day meekly accepting her fate, she decided. She would
type up the letters, send them off, and then order a
taxi to take her to the nearest train station or, if worse
came to worst, the bus station. And the sooner she
shook the dust of this place, the better.

The massive, earth-shaking thunder wrenched her
from a deep, troubled sleep. The gentle wind had
turned into a gale, slamming the French doors open
and whipping through her room like a relentless
cleaning lady, scooping up the sheaf of loose papers
by her bed and hurling them into the night air outside.
The thin lace curtains flapped against the open doorway, soaked by the sudden torrential downpour.

After another deafening clap of thunder, the light
Cassie had left burning went out, along with the dim
light outside on the rain-swept veranda. In the sudden
inky darkness Cassie saw the pale white paper fluttering in the wind, and without another moment's pause
she was out of bed and racing after her slaved-over
letter, oblivious to the rain-slick porch floor beneath
her feet or the soaking downpour that in seconds
plastered her thin cotton nightdress to her body and
drenched her long flowing hair.

As she struggled in the pitch darkness for the elusive paper, her bare feet slipped, and she felt herself falling toward the low railing that ran along the edge of the veranda. She watched herself as if from a distance, knowing full well that the momentum of her body precluded any chance of saving herself—knowing that the slate terrace was directly below her room and would no doubt be the end of her. She recognized it all quite calmly, reaching out with one last, futile attempt to break her fall as she hit the railing with her thighs.

Cassie felt her body tip dizzyingly over the edge, and then strong hands dug into the tender flesh of her upper arms, and she was dragged back to the warm, solid safety of a bare male chest. Bran's arms went around her trembling body and held her in a crushing grip that told her, along with his racing heartbeat beneath her head, that he had been as terrified as she was. Instinctively her arms went around his lean waist, reveling in the feel of his smooth wet skin, and for long countless moments she gave herself up to the warm haven of his embrace.

His flesh was smooth against her cheek in the torrid darkness. One strong hand cradled her head against his chest, and it would take only the tiniest fraction of an inch to press her mouth against that silky enticing skin. Just a small, almost involuntary movement, she thought dazedly, her heart pounding. It would hardly be her fault, and he probably wouldn't even notice.

Slowly, daringly, she made that small, imperceptible movement that brought her mouth against his chest. The skin was warm and wet and slightly salty to her shyly questing tongue. The scent of him, the sheer animal smell of heat and rain and a warm clean body, assailed her like a drug and combined with the taste of him to drive her to a senseless, prideless passion. She was totally unprepared for the strength of his reaction. An involuntary tremor shook his strong body_at the first tentative touch of her tongue, and he groaned, deep and low.

"Don't do that," he whispered harshly, his hand pressing her more fiercely against his chest.

"Why not?" she whispered in return, no longer amazed at her own boldness. In the dark rain-swept night all rules were suspended. The feel of his skin beneath her hands and mouth was too intoxicating to allow her usual firm control to reign. Her mouth traveled down to the small triangle of hair on his chest, her lips catching the little tendrils and tugging gently. "Why not?" she murmured again.

His hand slid down and caught her neck in an iron grip that was nonetheless gentle as he pulled her away, leaving his hips still pressed tightly against hers.

"Because of this," he uttered harshly, and his mouth caught hers.

Cassie was unprepared for the warm wet sweetness of his kiss, the taste of brandy and rain, the gently searching power of his tongue, as he sought out and received her response. There was no fight in her this time—only a desperate need to join with him, to be one with his powerful lean body. The rain continued to pour down on their entwined figures, but not even a flood could have quenched the stubborn flame of passion that flared between the two of them. Slowly, reluctantly, Bran's mouth left hers. One arm was still around her, his hand on the small of her back, pressing her against the tangible evidence of his desire, the tight jeans leaving nothing to her imagination. His other hand cupped the side of her neck, the thumb gently stroking her jawline, while he placed deliciously lingering kisses on each fluttering eyelid.

Lightning split the sky, followed by a deafening crack of thunder that seemed to shake the ground beneath Cassie's feet. And then the world swung crazily about her as she felt her wet trembling body being scooped up in Bran's strong arms and held high against his chest. For a moment she fought against his strong, restraining arms, but only for a moment. As he carried her in out of the pouring rain, she slid her arms around his neck, burying her face against his shoulder. With deceptive gentleness he laid her down on the bed, then tried to pull away. Her arms tightened in protest around his neck, pulling his willing body down to her.

"Don't leave me," she whispered. "Please."

Very gently he loosened her hands and placed them by her side. His large strong hands came up to frame her face. "I'm just going to close the French doors," he said softly. "We'll be soaked."

A small reluctant laugh escaped Cassie's throat. "We already are," she murmured, pulling him down again.

"So we are," he agreed, the laughter in his voice echoing hers, and the mattress sagged beneath his weight. With one hand going to either side of her waiting body, he leaned down, his face inches from hers, his breath warm and sweet on her damp skin. "I

should get you a towel," he murmured, not moving.
"You'll catch pneumonia."

She lay there, waiting. In the inky blackness she
could barely make out his expression, and she was
glad. She didn't want to risk seeing that sensual
mouth, which could kiss her into oblivion, curled in
contempt; didn't want to risk seeing the light of lust
and nothing else in those devastating silver-blue eyes.
With sudden blinding clarity she realized she wanted
to see something more—wanted to see warmth and
tenderness and affection along with desire. And, yes,
she wanted to see love reflected in those eyes, reflect-
ing hers.

While lying motionless she waited, closing her eyes
to the disillusionment that awaited her, closing her
eyes to sanity and doubt. For the first time in her life
she was a helpless prey to her own desires and the
tightly leashed passion of the man leaning over her. If
he moved away to get her a towel, moved away for
even a moment, sanity would return, and she could
order him from her bedroom and her bed with cold
disdain. She waited, breathless for the outcome, determined to do nothing to influence it one way or the
other. For once in her life she had willingly sur-
rendered control, and there was nothing she would do
until Bran made his move.

There was a slow, decisive expelling of air above
her, and the warm breath fanned her face as his hands
left the bed and slid up her arms. "The hell with the
towel," he muttered thickly. "I can warm you faster."

With mingled relief and regret she lifted her mouth
to meet his, opening it beneath the demanding heat of

his thrusting tongue. While his mouth was caught in a torrent of desire with hers, his hands were deftly stripping the sodden nightgown from her slender body, brushing against her sensitized flesh and stirring the desire that burned in her loins to a conflagration. And then his mouth left hers, blazing a trail down the line of her jaw, resting for a delightful, lingering moment on the hollow at the base of her throat, then moving downward in concert with the strong warming hands that caressed her flesh, the chilled aroused flesh that now lay bared to his knowing hands. Agonizingly slowly his tongue traced concentric circles around her hardened nipple while his hand cupped her other pale breast. Cassie slid her hands into Bran's thick dark hair, down his smooth broad shoulders and leanly muscled back, her fingers playing lightly over the sleek warm hide of him. A low moan in the back of Bran's throat signaled his approval as he moved his hungry mouth to her other breast. His hand was traveling down her soft warm skin, his slightly callused fingers brushing across her stomach, trailing down to reach the silken heat of her.

Letting out a small gasp of shock and pleasure, Cassie dug her fingers into his back, arching her hips mutely to reach that hand.

"Oh, you like that, do you?" he murmured against her breast. "And what else do you like, Cassie? Do you like this?" Another moan of pleasure escaped her lips, and she pulled him closer to her straining body. "And this?" Another sigh. "And what about this?"

A low agonized wail came from somewhere in the back of her throat as her body dissolved into a thou-

sand windblown petals. Slowly she drifted back, back
to her bed, to the man lying beside her. Distantly she
heard the sound of wet denim being removed, and
then he was above her, gently parting her legs, poised
and ready as his hands cupped her face.

"I can't wait any longer," Bran whispered gently,
his lips brushing hers. "I've wanted you for too long.
This past week has been torture for me. You knew
that, didn't you?" At her almost imperceptible nod
he brushed her lips again, more lingeringly. "Since
the first moment I saw you at the airport I've wanted
you, burned for you. And you've wanted me, haven't
you?" She tried to nod again, but his hands held her
immobile. "Haven't you?" he repeated. "I want to
hear you say it. I need to hear you say it." Was there a
note of pleading in his low, sensual voice? Surely not,
she thought. A man like Bran Rathburne would never
plead.

"I want you," she whispered against his mouth,
her voice blurred and husky. "I think I've always
wanted you. Please, Bran. Now."

"Now," he agreed, and slowly, gently yet firmly,
he completed their union, driving deep into her welcoming desire, reveling in the sudden tiny cry of fulfillment that came from her lips.

Together they moved in perfect rhythm, the white-
hot flame of their desire burning hotter. Cassie was
engulfed by his strong demanding body, engulfed and
strengthened until she felt the passion mount out of
control once more. And then suddenly, unexpectedly,
she exploded in a shimmering mass of sensation,
drifting through space, but this time not alone. Bran

was with her, in her arms, in her body, shuddering with the culmination of their passion until he was still, lying exhausted against her.

Once more she gave in to impulse, turning her mouth against his sweat-slick skin. Light rain was still blowing through the open French doors, and intermittent gusts of wind splattered their entwined bodies. Slowly he moved from her, collapsing beside her in exhaustion. She started to edge away, but an iron hand caught her arm, pulling her against him, spoon-fashion, as he flipped a sheet over their rapidly chilling bodies. She could feel his mouth just behind her ear, planting a light, lingering kiss that tingled her somnolent nerve endings.

"Bran..." she began, her voice husky and weak.

"Sssh." His mouth moved to her shoulder. "Sleep now, Cassie. We have plenty of time to talk tomorrow." He pulled her close against the warm lean strength of him, and Cassie gave up the struggle. In truth, there was no place she would rather be at that moment, and she was far too tired to let her better judgment regain control. Leaning back against him, she gave in to sleep.

Chapter Ten

Sunshine was streaming through the open French
doors, sparkling the damp rugs with light, drying the
rain-drenched curtains that still flapped wetly in the
soft spring breeze. Slowly, very slowly, Cassie opened
her eyes, then shut them again. She didn't want to wake
up, didn't want to move from this gloriously comfortable cocoon of blankets. Her body felt warm, sated, and
slightly sore in unexpected places, but apart from that
she felt more at peace with herself than she had in what
seemed like years. And then memory flooded back
with the strong sunshine, and as her eyes flew open and
her face turned crimson, she realized that the soreness
wasn't the least unexpected—not after a night like the
last one. It had been almost three years since her last
relationship, and in that time she had steered clear of
any involvements, emotional, physical, or both.

But not anymore. Tentatively she stretched out a
foot, encountering nothing behind her. Steeling herself, she sat up to face an empty bed, the imprint of
Bran's head still on the pillow beside her, the rumpled
sheets and sodden jeans on the floor attesting to the

activities of the night before. With a nervous little sigh Cassie leaned back against the pillows, still not quite sure of her reactions. Bran must have gone to his own bedroom sometime in the early hours of the morning, not even bothering to retrieve his clothes. But why hadn't he woken her up? she wondered. She had promised Meredith she'd be in by nine o'clock this morning. It had to be later than that. . . .

The sight of the small travel alarm by her bed put a stop to her rambling thoughts. Unbelievably, it read twenty-five past twelve.

It took her a record seven minutes to jump in the shower, throw on a pair of jeans and a thin cotton sweater, and race down to the kitchen, leaving her bedroom, bed, and the bathroom in a shambles. She was still braiding her damp hair when she ran smack into Mrs. Bellingson.

"You're up, then," the older woman greeted her, handing her a cup of coffee automatically. "Bran said I wasn't to wake you, though, personally, I think he was wrong. Even if the storm kept you up all night, I would have thought you'd want to get in early to see Meredith. But you know men—there's no reasoning with them sometimes." She sighed.

Cassie scalded her tongue, taking a hasty gulp of the coffee. "Have you heard how she's doing this morning?"

"Getting stronger and better every hour. The operation's been declared a complete success, of course. And a great relief it is for the whole family. She's been restless, now that she's finally decided to get better. Been asking for you all morning."

"And I promised to be there early," she mourned. "How can I get to the hospital? Is Bran coming back to get me?"

A troubled look darkened the housekeeper's face for a brief moment. "No, dearie. He had to take off on a last-minute business trip up north. He waited just long enough to make sure she was still doing all right and then he had to leave."

"Leave?" Cassie echoed, a curious feeling of fatality settling down over her. "What could be so important that he'd have to run off like that when Meredith needs him most?"

"I can't imagine, but Bran wouldn't go unless it was absolutely necessary. Listen, I don't think Gary will be wanting to leave the hospital to come back and get you. Why don't you take my car and go see her? I won't need it till six o'clock, and if you're still at the hospital, I can always have my husband pick me up. How does that sound?"

"Wonderful," Cassie breathed, draining the last of the scalding coffee and grabbing the proffered keys.

"And don't speed!" Mrs. Bellingson warned as Cassie raced out the door. "We don't want another car accident to break our hearts."

Despite Mrs. Bellingson's admonition Cassie fairly tore down the winding dirt roads that fed into secondary paved roads and then into thruways on her dash to the hospital, all the time keeping her eyes alert for a sight of Bran's silver Jaguar. Not that she would say or do anything if she did see him. She could scarcely flag him down, jump out of Mrs. Bellingson's lumbering

American car, and say "I just wanted to make sure you didn't regret last night."

She could well imagine how those silver-blue eyes would stare down at her, cool disdain and perhaps triumphant amusement hidden in their depths. If he'd wanted revenge for her supposed ill-treatment of Meredith, if he wanted power over her, surely the hours last night when she lay quivering in his arms satisfied both those longings. Did he have any other longings she could satisfy? she wondered.

God, how could she have been such a fool last night? And how could she be such a fool right now, to long for him till she thought she might explode? she asked herself. Her body still tingled from his remembered touch. Her skin still flamed from the lingering memory of his hungry mouth. How could he have made love to her, worshiped her body with all the power and passion in his strong frame, for no other reason than temporary lust? She'd had lust alone in the past, and there was a world of difference between other men's savage gropings and the bone-shattering delight she'd felt with Bran last night. But was there a difference for Bran?

"What are you doing here?" Gary's glowering visage was her first greeting as she dashed into the hushed spotless confines of the hospital. "I didn't think you were going to bother to show up at all, despite your protestations of caring for Meredith. Bran and I have been here since seven, while you picked this morning to sleep in. She's been asking for you for hours now!"

Ignoring his hostility had become a habit by now.

Cassie went straight to the heart of the matter. "Is Bran with her now?"

"He left a short while ago for Princeton." There was a gleam of triumph in Gary's angry eyes, and Cassie's stomach knotted.

"Princeton?" she echoed. "Why?"

"I have no idea. I assume it has something to do with you."

It was all Cassie could do to banish the sudden upsurge of guilt that flooded her. She had done nothing wrong, despite the fact that all evidence would lead Bran to think the opposite. Deliberately she turned her attention to matters closer to hand. "How is Meredith? Mrs. Bellingson said she's feeling stronger all the time. Is she sitting up and talking? Does she want visitors?"

"I would suppose so. I haven't seen her." The bitterness was strong in his voice, and his eyes were like chips of green ice.

"For heaven's sake, why not?" she demanded impatiently.

"Because she refuses to see me, just as she's refused to see me since she came back from Princeton. Thanks, I'm sure, to you," he shot back. "Well, you can tell her for me that I won't bother her anymore. She doesn't have to worry that I'll chase after her, trying to change her mind. As long as she's going to be okay, that's all I care about. Tell her I love her and that I always will. I'm leaving now, and—"

"Oh, for pity's sake!" Cassie grabbed his arm, harassed beyond endurance. "You're not going anywhere, do you hear me? You can stop being so damn noble, and Meredith can stop being so damn stupid. The two of you give me a pain. You have everything going for you, you love each other, and you manufacture obstacles. When I think of what real obstacles are like, I'd like to bash your heads together."

"I'm not manufacturing a thing. Meredith and I were engaged to be married, but she wanted to try living on her own for a year. And then she met you and decided she wanted to be a career woman like you and that I could go fly a kite."

"Is that what she told you?" Cassie's voice was level.

"She didn't tell me a thing. She handed me back my ring, said it wouldn't work, and refused to speak to me again."

After casting a harried glance about her, Cassie spied a small waiting room a few yards down the hall from Meredith's room. "All right," she said evenly. "I'm going to see Meredith, and you're going to sit in that waiting room until I'm finished."

"The hell I am—" he started to object, but Cassie turned on him, her five feet nine inches bristling with barely restrained fury.

"Listen, you stupid jerk," she hissed. "You and Bran have spent this last week griping and moaning about how I have all this power over Meredith, how I can make her do anything I want, and what a horrible influence I am on her. Well, for one damn moment why don't you let me try to use my supposed wicked influence to make her see reason? Or isn't she worth any more effort?"

His green eyes met her furious brown ones for a

long thoughtful moment. "I'll be in the waiting
room," he said quietly.

Like a warrior going into battle, Cassie sailed into
Meredith's hospital room. Meredith looked much better than she had directly after the surgery. She was
sitting up, a spot of fresh color on either pale cheek,
her blue eyes clear.

She smiled up at her visitor with pathetic eagerness.
"Cassie, where have you been? I thought you were
never coming," she said plaintively. "Bran said you
weren't feeling well, but I couldn't believe you'd let
me down. I knew you wouldn't."

It was all Cassie could do to steel herself against the
puppy-dog expression in Meredith's face. "I'm sorry
I'm late, Meredith. But you had a lot of caring people
here waiting to see you." She sat in the straight chair
beside the bed and took Meredith's thin hand in her
strong, capable one.

"Yes, Bran's been here since early this morning,"
she agreed.

"I wasn't talking about Bran."

A shadow crossed Meredith's face. "The staff has
been marvelous, too. Dr. Haughey is one of the
best—"

"I wasn't talking about the medical staff, either,
Meredith," she said sternly. "There are other people
here who love you very much."

"There's you, and there's Bran," she said stubbornly.

"And there's Gary."

"I don't want to talk about him." She tried to pull
her hand out of Cassie's stronger one, to no avail.

"Tough," she said unsympathetically. "He's been haunting these corridors for the last week, desperate for a glimpse of you, for word that you're on the mend, and you've refused to give him the slightest bit of comfort. I sincerely hope you have a good reason for putting someone as nice as he is through such misery." Cassie was only guessing that underneath his pugnacious attitude lay a heart of gold. Meredith must have had some reason for getting engaged to him in the first place.

"He isn't nice!" Meredith shot back. "He called you a gold-digging, immoral bitch and said that I shouldn't have anything to do with you."

For a moment Cassie was taken aback, and then her sense of humor reasserted itself. "Is that all?" she said wryly. "Your brother has said far worse things, and I don't see you banishing him from your life."

"Bran's said things like that?"

"That, and much worse. I've come to accept the fact, Meredith, that the evidence is damning. I can't blame anyone for jumping to the conclusion that I cheated on the research, with people like Stanley Alleyn and Dr. Thompson accusing me. Even one of my best friends was prepared to believe the worst of me." It was a low blow, calculated to have a strong effect, and as Meredith's huge eyes filled with tears, Cassie knew she'd hit home.

"But I knew I was wrong! The moment I thought about it, I knew you could never have done such a thing!" she wailed.

"Of course you did. But Bran and Gary don't know me at all. How could you expect them to believe me innocent when they had no knowledge of my sterling character?'' she injected lightly, a small smile tugging at the corners of her mouth. "But that's not the real reason you gave Gary back his ring, is it?''

"Of course it is!" she said weakly.

"It is not. And I'd like you to tell me why. I think you owe it to me, Meredith, and I think you owe it to him. You must have some better reason for destroying a man like Gary.''

"Destroying?'' she echoed, puzzled.

"Of course. He loves you, you idiot. I think he'd do anything for you.''

The last bit of restraint vanished from Meredith's weakened body. "But that's the problem!" she wailed. "I don't deserve him. I tried to tell him that, but he wouldn't listen. He's so good to me, and I know I'd only betray him and let him down the same way I let you down. I don't know how to keep house very well, I'd probably be too scatterbrained to be a good mother, and I can't even be loyal. He's better off without me...." Her voice trailed off into loud sobs.

Cassie watched her friend for a long silent moment as she snuffled noisly into a tissue. When the storm of emotion had temporarily abated, she spoke.

"Meredith, for someone so frighteningly bright, you are incredibly stupid sometimes. Everyone lets people down sometimes. It's part of life, and people get over it—if there's love between them. It's far worse to deliberately hurt someone out of cowardice and fear of life than to let him down by accident.''

Meredith's tear-drenched eyes met hers. "But I'm

afraid, Cassie," she whispered. "I don't know if I'm strong enough."

"It's hard to be strong alone. It's much easier when there are two of you. He's waiting down the hall. Shall I go out and tell him to go home, or shall I have him come in?"

"Will you stay with me?" she begged piteously.

Cassie shook her head. "This is something the two of you have to work out alone. You have a good chance of making it, Meredith. It's worth the effort—don't throw it away." Slowly she rose, heading for the door. "Which is it to be?"

"Does he really want to see me?" There was pitiful hope in her voice.

"He was about to leave when I got here, and he told me to tell you that he loved you and always would. Considering that he's been wandering these hallways like a lost soul for the last week, I would certainly think he'd like to see you."

Meredith took a deep breath and squared her shoulders. Her black hair tumbled down her shoulders, her face was pale and shadowed from the surgery, and her eyes were red and swollen from her recent weeping. But a spark of hope had somehow come alive, and she looked prettier than Cassie had ever seen her. "Ask him to come in, please," Meredith said firmly.

Chapter Eleven

Cassie's euphoria lasted well into the evening. She had taken the long way home from the hospital, traveling through the countryside at a leisurely pace, doing her best to dwell on Meredith and Gary and not to wonder why in the world Bran would suddenly find it necessary to race off to Princeton. Mrs. Bellingson had greeted her at the front door with the news that Meredith, wonder of wonders, had just called to announce that she and Gary were getting married after all, in two weeks time.

A bottle of Bran's Moët champagne was called for, quickly iced, and drained in celebration. By the time Mrs. Bellingson's long-suffering husband had come to fetch her, Cassie and her cohort were weaving slightly and feeling no pain. They had determined that she would leave her car for Cassie, and it was just as well. Neither of them was in any shape to get behind the wheel that afternoon.

There had been only one shadow to mar the celebration. Cassie had been doing her best to ignore the slightly troubled look in Mrs. Bellingson's mild eyes.

A trip to her bedroom had revealed that the house-keeper, true to form, had cleaned up after her. She had made the tumbled bed, removed Bran's sodden jeans from the floor, and effectively banished any sign of last night's occupation from the room. She'd even put fresh sheets on the bed.

Cassie, who had seldom been a coward, was the first to broach the subject. "Thank you for straightening my room," she said evenly. "I'm sorry I left it in such a mess, but I was in a hurry to get to the hospital." She met Mrs. Bellingson's eyes candidly, and the older woman's expression softened.

"I don't want you to get hurt, dearie," she said gently, going straight to the heart of the matter. "I've grown very fond of you the last few days. I wouldn't want you to get in over your head. I'm not really sure what's on Bran's mind nowadays. For a while I was afraid he was going to marry Lucy Barrow, but in the last few weeks he's been seeing less of her. Even before you came. But I don't know if he's ready to make any sort of commitment right now. And I think I know you too well to imagine that you've gone into this with a casual attitude."

Cassie drained her glass, reaching out to refill it and Mrs. Bellingson's at the same time. "No, you're right. And there's no telling what's going to happen, now that Meredith's better. I imagine his sudden business trip has something to do with me. I'll just have to see what happens whenever he returns."

"That'll be tomorrow," Mrs. Bellingson supplied, and Cassie felt her control slipping somewhat. "He called just before Meredith did, saying he'd be back late in the afternoon and that I was to take the day off. Of course, I'll be glad to come in if you need me...."

"Heavens, no. I'll be just fine." Cassie lied through her teeth. The farmhouse could be very empty.

"I suppose you could fill in the time by visiting Meredith," she suggested with a trace of doubt.

"And I would imagine that I would be just slightly in the way," Cassie said with a grin. "I think the two of them will have eyes and ears for no one but themselves. And I should start making plans to head back home. I don't think Meredith will even notice whether I'm here or not." She kept her tone deliberately cheerful, but Mrs. Bellingson wasn't fooled.

"You won't do anything hasty, now, dearie?" she admonished. "You'll wait till Bran gets back?"

"Oh, yes," Cassie sighed. "I'll wait."

But the afternoon that had started so promisingly stretched into an endless barren wasteland. Studiously Cassie avoided the smaller living room with its brandy, its sultry records, and the far too comfortable sofa. Despite her nervous craving for food she avoided the kitchen and refrigerator for the same reason. And the last thing she wanted to do was crawl all alone into her bed when her body and soul ached for him. She compromised by sitting in the front living room, her wandering mind paying absolutely no attention to the violent movie on television. And it was there that she fell asleep, still dressed in the jeans and cotton sweater she'd thrown on that morning.

Perhaps it was the sudden silence that alerted her. Or some part of her sleeping mind felt his silver-blue eyes on her curled-up form. Slowly she opened her eyes in the darkened room. He'd turned off the television and most of the lights and stood towering over her. In the dim light his expression was unreadable.

She stared up at him without saying a word. The windows were still open, and she could hear the soft steady beat of the gentle rain that was falling, feel the warm damp spring breeze that caressed her heated skin. She felt as if she were frozen in time, doomed to eternity with this mesmerizing, bewitching, frightening man looming over her—to berate her, to make love to her, she couldn't guess which, and couldn't decide which would be the greater relief.

Finally, he spoke, "I wasn't sure you'd still be here," he said coldly, and each clipped word was like an icicle in her heart.

"Why wouldn't I be?" Her voice came out low and a bit more shaky than she would have liked, but calm enough, given the circumstances.

"You've fulfilled your part of the bargain. You've stayed until Meredith is finally getting better. You managed to keep from interfering with her life long enough for her and Gary to get back together."

"Where did you hear that from?" she questioned coolly. "I rather thought I'd done a great deal of interfering."

"I stopped and saw Meredith on my way back from the airport. She was still so excited, she could barely sleep, and most of what she said made little sense. The one thing that was clear was that she and Gary had patched things up, no thanks to you, I'm sure."

It's only my pride that's hurt, she warned herself cautiously as she moved into a sitting position. Bran still towered over her like an avenging god, and she could see then how tired he was. His beautiful eyes were shadowed with exhaustion, and his mouth was thin and harsh with emotions Cassie couldn't even begin to guess at. All of them negative, no doubt, she thought.

"I can leave tomorrow," she said quietly. "I wanted to wait and discuss it with you."

"Why?" The single word was uncompromisingly cruel, and it was all Cassie could do to keep from hurling it back in his teeth.

"Because we made a bargain." Her voice was calm as she swung her legs from underneath her and set her bare feet on the cool oak floor. "I kept my part of it. Are you going to keep your part of it?"

He moved then, sinking down into a nearby chair in utter weariness, the only energy about him a simmering rage that reached across the room like an angry storm. "I wouldn't have said you kept it totally. Meredith tells me that you said I called you all sorts of names. She demanded to know how I could treat you so cruelly." There was a sneer in his voice.

"I—I'm sorry. I shouldn't have told her that. It happened to slip out."

"I'm sure it did. So you expect me to honor the bargain, help you find a new job, despite the fact that you not only tried to drive a wedge between my sister and me but you lied and cheated on crucial research, with absolutely no sign of guilt or compunction—"

"For heaven's sake, I didn't!" she cried, harassed. "I've tried to tell you any number of times. I had nothing to do with the falsified data, I swear to you...."

"You needn't bother," he drawled. "You could swear up and down, and I still wouldn't believe you. Where do you think I was today?"

"At the Thompson Nutri-Center," she said dully. "Gary said you'd gone to Princeton."

"And what do you think I discovered there?"

"You tell me, though I can well imagine. Probably a pack of lies, well documented. What I don't understand is why you suddenly felt you had to race up there," Cassie said with a trace of asperity. "Was it because after making love to me you decided I couldn't be quite so wretched?" There, it was out in the open, the subject they'd both been studiously avoiding.

"Making love?" he mocked. "Is that what you call it? I would have used another word." And the word he used was short and crude and cruel.

Cassie leaped to her feet, her fury suddenly surpassing his. "I don't have to listen to you," she said in a clipped tone of voice. "Your opinion was already far too clear. You won't believe a word I say and you won't hold to your part of the agreement. Well, that's just fine. I wouldn't want your damn help. I'd rather do it on my own. You can be assured I'll be out of here the first thing tomorrow."

"No, you won't." His voice stopped her as she stormed toward the door. "You aren't going anywhere."

"Try and stop me," she spat back, slamming out of the room with a combination of rage and panic that had her heart racing beneath the thin cotton sweater.

Bran caught her halfway up the stairs, his strong
tanned hands reaching out and imprisoning her against
his broad chest. She could feel his heart racing in time
with hers, feel his rapid breathing stirring her hair.
"You aren't going anywhere," he said again, pain and
desire raw in his voice. "Except to bed with me." He
pulled away, and his eyes glittered down into hers in
the darkness. "Aren't you?" The question was soft,
as soft as his lips as he brushed her trembling mouth.
"Aren't you?"

"Why, Bran?" she whispered helplessly against the
teasing pressure of his sweet wet mouth.

"Because you want me and need me, almost as
much as I want and need you." She tried to shake her
head, to deny the all too apparent truth of his claim,
but his hand caught her chin in a firm, uncompromis-
ing grip, even as his thumb stroked her sensitive
jawline. "Don't lie to me, Cassie. Don't lie to me anymore." There was a note of pleading in his husky
voice, a note she could no more resist than she could
fly.

"Yes," she said helplessly. "Yes, yes, yes."

He scooped her up in his arms effortlessly, holding
her high against his chest. His thin linen shirt was
damp beneath her clutching fingers, damp from the
steady stream of rain that echoed around them.

Cassie gave up the last vestiges of protest, resting
her head against that strong, comforting shoulder as
he carried her higher and higher. She could still feel
the last traces of anger wound tight inside him, and
knew that she should tell him to put her down, to
leave her alone.

They were in his darkened bedroom, the door kicked shut behind them, and he was placing her down gently on the bed before she realized she had no intention of leaving him that night. Some things were worth fighting for, worth risking pain and cruel hurt and disillusionment for. And from the moment Cassie had awakened to find him glowering down at her, she had recognized what she should have seen days ago. She was in love with him, deeply, desperately in love with him. And that love made no sacrifice, no risk, too great.

Bran followed her down onto the king-size bed, his hands rough and hurried as they pulled away her clothes. Her sweater was yanked none too gently over her head, her jeans unzipped and stripped from her willing body. The rough urgency in him communicated itself to her, and she attacked his clothes with equal fervor, desperate for the feel of his warm muscled chest against her tender breasts. In a moment they were both naked, the final barriers down between them, alone in the dark, all misunderstandings vanished, all doubts and fears receded. As his wet hungry mouth closed over one pouting breast, she let out a small moan of surrender.

"You don't know how I've longed to hear that," he whispered against her skin, his tongue trailing teasing concentric circles around the aroused nipple. "All day long that sound has haunted me. That soft sweet sighing sound you make when I'm pleasuring you. I don't know how I stood it," he groaned, and his mouth trailed soft damp kisses down the warm smooth skin of her stomach, his tongue stopping long enough to caress her navel until she thought she would go mad with pleasure.

"Bran," she begged as his mouth moved lower. "Please."

He kissed her slender thighs, his warm breath making her tremble uncontrollably. "You're so damn beautiful, Cassie. I've dreamed about doing this all day. Let me hear you make those sounds again," he grated against the tender flesh of her inner thigh. "Let me hear you moan and weep in surrender." And his mouth found her, his tongue hot and bold as his hands cupped her buttocks, cradling her as he brought her to the edge of fulfillment and beyond.

"Bran," she cried, her heels digging into the mattress, her fingers laced through his curly black hair as the tears coursed down her face. And then he moved up and covered her, driving into her with all his fierce, yet tender strength, as his hands reached up to cup her face and his mouth kissed away her tears.

He held still within her as his mouth gently nipped at her eyelids, her lips, her earlobes, waiting until her final, shuddering spasms had passed, and still he seemed content to lie there, tasting her tears, until Cassie could bear it no longer and arched her hips up against him.

A low seductive laugh rumbled deep in his chest. "Insatiable creature," he murmured in her ear. "I thought you'd need more time to recover."

She smiled up at him, secure in the knowledge that he couldn't see the love shining in her eyes. "I don't think I could ever get enough of you," she whispered softly.

"The feeling is mutual," he said, setting his mouth on hers with a kind of savage hunger that nevertheless held a basic underlying tenderness. As his tongue ravished her mouth their bodies followed suit, until they once more scaled the mountainous ledges of desire, tumbling over the precipice into an abyss of sated passion that left them trembling in each others' arms.

I can't ever leave him, she thought with a possessive fierceness as she held him cradled against her, felt his breathing and heartbeat slowly return to normal. *Not unless he drives me away. I love him too much.*

As if he could read her thoughts he stirred, withdrawing from her and moving to lie on his back beside her, staring up at the ceiling with unseeing eyes. For a long lonely moment Cassie felt bereft, rejected, and then his hand reached out and caught hers lightly, the thumb caressing her palm in a slow lazy movement.

"I covered for you," he said quietly, his thumb keeping up its mesmerizing rhythm.

Cassie stirred sleepily. "Covered for me?" she echoed uncomprehendingly.

"With the Nutri-Center. I told Thompson if he didn't destroy the incriminating lab work and give you a clean recommendation, then the Rathburne Foundation would have to start looking for another project to fund." There was bitter self-mockery in his voice in the darkened room.

Cassie was wide awake by this point, her nerves tingling. "Bran, I promise you. I didn't falsify those research results. Someone else must have, probably Dr. Alleyn." She begged for him to trust her, believe in her.

"Cassie, I don't want to hear it," he said wearily. "It was all there in black and white—the evidence was irrefutable. But you don't have to worry. It's been destroyed. A little corporate blackmail does wonders."

A cold bleakness settled over her heart. "Why, Bran?" she asked flatly. "Why did you do it?"

His eyes as he turned to look at her were unreadable in the dim light. "It was the only way I could think of to bribe you into staying."

"Staying?"

"Here, with me," he explained patiently. "I don't want you to leave me. Heaven knows why," he added with brutal frankness.

"Heaven knows why," she echoed bitterly. "You don't trust me. You don't seem even to like me."

"I don't," he agreed with final, heart-shattering honesty. "But for some damn reason I seem to be falling in love with you."

The words that a few moments ago would have filled her with ecstasy sealed the coffin of her heart. Cassie lay still, the pain too great to hurt.

"You're telling me that despite the dislike and contempt you have for me, you think you love me," she repeated, not quite believing his words. "And what will the board of directors at the Foundation think of your blackmail?"

"They won't like it. With any luck they won't have to find out. I'd have a hell of a time explaining," he said wearily. His voice was heavy with the sleeplessness and exhaustion of the last few days. "But you're going to stay." It was a statement, not a question.

"There'll be something you can do in the area—some project at the university."

Cassie didn't even hesitate. "No, Bran."

He turned on his side, pulling her slender, suddenly chilled body against the warmth of his flesh. "We'll talk about it tomorrow," he murmured in her ear, his mouth placing a last, lingering kiss on the slender column of her neck.

"No, Bran," she said again. But he was already asleep.

She spent the night with him. At one point in the small hours of the morning she tried to disentangle herself from his possessive embrace, but he woke and pulled her back, making love to her with a sweet fierceness that broke her heart all over again. When the first rays of fitful sunshine filtered into the room, she made her escape, stopping long enough to stare down at his sleeping form, as if to memorize everything about him. His curly black hair was rumpled around his head, and with the harsh lines of anger and weariness relaxed in sleep, he looked ten years younger and infinitely dear. Resolutely, silently, she closed the door behind her.

Cassie didn't even pause long enough for a shower. She had no desire to wash the scent and feel of him from her skin—she wanted to treasure it for as long as she could. Pulling on her jeans and her sweater over fresh underwear, she threw the rest of her clothes into her duffel bag. The house was silent as she crept down the winding staircase. Ten minutes later the taxi arrived at the far end of the driveway, and she was gone.

Chapter Twelve

Sandra Thayer leaned her slender back against the thick upholstery and stared across the neat expanse of her desk toward the defiantly open window. It was a blustery day for May second, with just a nip in the air, but she never let her birthday go by without paying this small homage to spring and a new year. And on this, her thirtieth birthday, she wasn't about to break the precedent. An uneasy feeling at the back of her neck warned her she'd need all the good fortune a capricious providence felt like showering upon her.

Sighing, she leaned forward, staring out at the wind-tossed blustery Oregon countryside. If she were home, perched atop her cliff in the wood-and-stone retreat that provided her haven and solace, she could sit and watch the waves crash against the rocks below, let the sea breeze take her sun-streaked brown hair and toss it about her shoulders, the damp salt air whipping color into her tanned face. Damn it, she should have taken the day off, she thought. People should be allowed to celebrate their birthdays in whatever way they wished, especially something as monumental as a thirtieth birthday. Instead she was trapped behind her usually welcome desk, a feeling of foreboding and restlessness threatening to take all pleasure out of the day.

And how could she possibly justify her restlessness, other than attributing it to spring fever? she asked herself. She could look back on her first thirty years with a sense of justifiable accomplishment, knowing that she had overcome seemingly insurmountable difficulties by sheer grit and determination to reach her present spot. She had a satisfying career as assistant head of research at the tiny well-respected Cooper Laboratories in Bern, Oregon, without even a trace of her shadowed past to mar the high esteem and affection in which she was held. She had her baby daughter, Merrie, round-faced and smiling and enchantingly lovely, and a comfortable, mutually satisfying relationship with David Tremayne, her coworker and immediate supervisor. Thankfully she worked with someone she could trust. Not like that other time...

Swiftly she put those unpleasant memories from her mind, rising from her chair and strolling toward the open window with its distant tang of sea air. A great deal had changed for her since that first abortive job. Cassandra O'Neill had become Sandra Thayer, taking her mother's maiden name. Her long, often braided chestnut hair had been cut to shoulder length and now swung free, streaked lightly by the fitful Oregon sunshine. Motherhood had ripened her slim boyish figure, giving her soft, delicious curves that no man had yet enjoyed. Her glasses, essentially useless, had been discarded, and there was a new serenity in her warm honey-brown eyes, with just a trace of distant sadness lingering in the background.

It had been an extremely difficult first few months. She had returned to Princeton long enough to collect her most easily transportable belongings and her repaired VW, bid a tearful but hasty farewell to Eliza, and taken off for Oregon. Her sister, June, was to provide her with a warm haven in which to lick her wounds and decide what she was going to do with the rest of her life.

But Merrie had put a stop to all that. Cassie hadn't been at her sister's for more than a month when the inevitable had to be faced. She was pregnant with Bran's child.

There was never any question in her mind as to what to do. She had training, a profession. She could find a job and support her child. And so it was that a young researcher, still lacking her Ph.D., four months pregnant, unmarried, with a completely tarnished reputation, had the gall to apply for the job as assistant head of research at the Cooper Laboratories, not fifteen miles from June's rambling ranch house.

And for once luck was with her. Dr. Gibson was a sympathetic, understanding elderly widower with a past acquaintance with and dislike for Stanley Alleyn. He had taken Sandra Thayer's word unquestioningly, waived the need for references and a completed thesis, and hired her on the spot. Neither of them had ever regretted the move, especially when the world of research was rocked a few months later by the dismissal of Stanley Alleyn from the world-famous

Thompson Nutri-Center. Cassie considered it a baby present, for that afternoon she went into labor and delivered a seven-pound baby girl.

It took her two full weeks of postpartum depression and struggling with her conscience to decide to let Bran know he was a father, however accidentally. Part of her argued that she owed him nothing. What had given him a few moments of pleasure had cost her nine months of discomfort and worry and twenty-three hours of hard, painful labor. But it was his child, her other self argued. The man had a right to know.

In the end fairness had won out. Steeling herself, she had waited until Merrie was sleeping soundly one evening, and had dialed Bran's phone number. Her heart was thumping so loudly in her breast that she could barely hear the distant ringing on the other side of the country, and her hands were trembling and slippery with sweat. She hadn't even begun to plan what she would say to him, how she would tell him. He had a right to know, but did it have to be so damn hard? she questioned.

"Hullo?" A sleepy, sultry female voice answered the phone, and Cassie realized with belated guilt that it must be after midnight in Virginia.

"Mrs. Bellingson?" she queried hesitantly.

"No, this is Lucy Barrow." The voice on the other end brightened with curiosity. "To whom am I speaking, please?"

Cassie tried one last time. "Is Bran there?" Her voice was thick with the oncoming tears that never seemed far away these days.

"Who's calling?" Lucy questioned again, snappish this time. "I'm not about to wake him except for a good reason."

Slowly, quietly, Cassie replaced the receiver in its cradle. It was more than clear—she'd been gone nine months. It was little wonder Bran had taken up where he'd left off with Lucy. If, indeed, he'd ever actually stopped seeing her during the too-short time Cassie lived in his house.

But he said he was falling in love with me, her stubborn self wailed. Well, he'd obviously recovered swiftly enough from that particular affliction. Doubtless he and Lucy were married—they might even be expecting a child of their own. Why did the idea of Lucy's flat stomach rounded with Bran's child fill her with such a sick loathing that she felt as if she might throw up? What good would jealousy do at this point?

Besides, she still called herself Lucy Barrow. So they weren't married—at least, not yet. But she was living with him. It was just as well Cassie had found out this soon. She'd tried to do her duty. But if he could forget her so soon, he could just as easily ignore an unexpected daughter.

It was more than time to close that chapter in her life, she decided. Later, when Merrie was older, she'd tell her a bit about her father. The good parts. But in the meantime it was time to go back to work. She and her baby needed the money, and June would provide admirable child care while she was gone.

She had just begun to pull herself together after that devastating blow when her luck did a turnaround.

Her house had been a stroke of a suddenly beneficial fate at a time when she most needed it. A retired couple from Seattle found their rock-bound ocean retreat a bit too remote, with their only neighbor half a mile down the road. They didn't want to sell the place, hoping their younger son might someday want it when he retired from the navy, and they didn't want it to stand idle. What they did want was to help out a struggling single parent with a minimal amount of money for rent and a need for solitude. Cassie and Merrie had been in the rambling stone-and-wood structure perched atop the cliffs for a year now, and it was home.

As Cassie stared out her office window she tried to shake the sense of impending doom that had haunted her all morning. It was probably just that stupid cocktail party, she thought. David had browbeaten her—very charmingly, of course—into entertaining a group of bigwigs from the East Coast. It was David's duty, among other things, to drum up funding for the avid coffers of Cooper Laboratories, and he would at this very moment be shepherding a distinctly boring group of laboratory equipment manufacturers, college professors, and fellow researchers through the spotless, impressive labs that housed Cooper's current field of interest, the Pharmacopoeia Project—a massive amount of research into the healing properties of herbs and plants. The need for concrete medical proof was enormous in a field riddled with folklore and conjecture. Cassie, with what she laughingly denounced as pure sexism, had been placed in charge of the floral studies, and her own particular favorite was the pansy. Heartsease, it was called, and promised all sorts of beneficial properties that Cassie had so far failed to document. It couldn't even provide its named property. Cassie would have done anything—distilled it, injected it, smoked it, or snorted it—if it promised to ease the ever-present nagging pain in her heart. But to no avail. She still kept a pot of deep violet pansies in her window, hoping against hope that they might heal her by osmosis.

So she had to entertain a dozen boring businessmen and professionals and their wives. She'd done it before and she'd do it again. It was tedious but hardly conducive to the little tendrils of clawing panic that were beginning to creep up on her.

"You're being ridiculous, Cassie," she said out loud, annoyed with her fancifulness. Perhaps it was just sexual tension, she pondered, leaning her head against the side of the window. She'd kept David a safe, comfortable distance from her bed, not sure whether she was ready for the total commitment that would entail. Maybe this restless, waiting feeling was simply her body's way of telling her she was ready. After all, at the advanced age of thirty she ought to be ready for a lover—not that she expected anyone could compare with her last one.

"Damn," she said out loud again. "I don't want to think about him, today of all days." It had been almost two years since she'd seen him, lost in exhausted sleep, and still his image floated into her mind when she least expected it. Tall and lean and darkly dangerous, his silver-blue eyes glowing with anger and desire, his mouth...

"Damn," she said again, turning back from her desk. Her daughter's round baby's face looked up from a porcelain frame, the silver-blue eyes a perfect match to those she'd rather forget.

But she obviously wasn't going to forget him. Not on today, of all days, her birthday, and two years to the day that she first set eyes on him. She'd simply have to do her best to get through the day, keeping Bran Rathburne's memory firmly at bay. And tonight, after all the guests were gone and Merrie was safely down for the night, she could start a fire in the fireplace, curl up on the sofa, and allow herself the rare indulgence of tears. And tomorrow she would go to bed with David.

Resolutely she reached for the phone and pressed the three digits of his interoffice number. His ever-patient secretary answered.

"David's been looking for you everywhere, Sandra," she replied to Cassie's question. "He's taken the latest horde into the labs, but you were supposed to meet up with them by ten to explain the flower experiments. It's ten fifteen, and I would guess he's ready to strangle you."

"I'd think so, too. I'm on my way. And Helen, would you leave a message for him? Just leave a note to tell him that I *will* go out with him tomorrow night, after all."

"Tomorrow night," Helen verified. "Though if you don't catch up with him, he's more likely to beat you than feed you."

"Aye, aye, sir."

But why didn't she want to leave her office? she

asked herself. She could hear the tread of a dozen or
so well-shod feet, hear the deep portentous tones all
businessmen seemed to communicate in. While running a nervous hand through her curtain of chestnut
hair, she fairly tumbled toward the door, yanking it
open just as David Tremayne was about to knock.

David was a handsome kindly man in his early
forties, with ten pounds he wanted to lose, less sandy
hair than he would have liked, and a cheerful, easygo-
ing manner that endeared him to all. Cassie barely had
a moment to respond to his warm smile before the
bottom of her world dropped out.

"Sandra, there you are. We decided to come looking for you, since you were playing hard to get," he
said in a teasing tone of voice. "Let me introduce
you to our visitors. This is George Hanson and Fred
Curtis of Labworks, Professor Harvey from the
Salem Laboratories, Bran Rathburne of the Rathburne Foundation, and Margaret Graham of Tupper
Industries. This is Sandra Thayer, my right hand and
second in command. She's in charge of the floral
studies, and I'm sure she'll be delighted to explain
her part of our undertaking." He prodded her gently,
his warm hazel eyes slightly quizzical at her blanched
complexion.

"Of—of course," she stammered, feeling as if
she'd been hit in the solar plexus. And yet, all of the
five visiting dignitaries had blank yet polite expres-
sions. There was no light of recognition in those
silver-blue eyes, no familiar curling of his thin sensuous mouth. Nervously Cassie reached out a hand to
push her curtain of hair aside, hoping her voice

wouldn't betray her. Her only hope was to carry this off, and then escape as fast as she could.

"I'd be delighted to, David," she said smoothly, using her best public relations voice. "If you'll come with me, I can take you through the west section of the labs, where we have our greenhouses. That's where we've been experimenting with the various plants and herbs that are a part of the Pharmacopoeia Project, and as you can see..." Automatic pilot took over as she led the way down the corridors, past rows of healthy plants. In the meantime her brain was working feverishly. Could he really not recognize her? Her hair was shorter, obscuring her face somewhat, and the sun streaks changed the color. Without her glasses she had taken to wearing a bit more makeup, just enough to play up her honey-brown eyes. She dressed differently, too, in more feminine clothes than when she had stayed in that rambling old farmhouse in Virginia. And she had a new name. Perhaps she might just get away with it.

Suddenly she realized that they were all staring at her. "I beg your pardon," she stammered, flushing nervously.

"Mr. Rathburne asked you a question, Sandra," David prompted gently, a worried line between his eyes.

"He did?" Cassie's voice came out in a nervous little squeak, and by accident she met the eyes that she had been avoiding. They looked right through her, bland and silver-blue and unrecognizing.

"I wondered how long a time period you allotted to each experiment." His voice was still the same, slightly husky and capable of melting her bones. How could she have missed it when he spoke to her a moment before? she wondered.

"I think David would be more qualified to answer that," she said evasively, suddenly desperate to escape. If she had to stand there any longer in the pool of those distant eyes, her tenuous control would vanish completely. "I'm afraid I have something urgent going on right now. If you would all excuse me.. " she murmured. Without waiting for the polite words of acquiescence from her audience she turned too quickly, her ankle twisted, the high heel of her thin sandal snapped, and she was catapulted into the nearest pair of male arms. There could be no doubt whose arms would be closest. Fate had once more turned on her.

Bran caught her and helped her regain her balance with impersonal efficiency, his hands light on her skin. But she pulled away as if burned, and managed a muffled thanks before she limped off. She could feel eyes burning into her slender back, and she had little doubt whose eyes they were. But did they know her? she wondered.

With shaking hands she locked her office door, sinking down into the soft leather chair and burying her head in her hands. What the devil was she going to do?

After the initial panic had passed, priorities quickly became established. If he did know her, if he had come here deliberately to see her, then she had to somehow keep Merrie away from him, she knew. She would have to tell him sooner or later—in the last fifteen months her conscience had told her that. *But, please, not right now,* she begged silently.

Her sister answered the phone on the fifth long ring. "June, I need your help," she said without preamble. "Can Merrie stay with you for a few days?"

"Of course she can. You know we love having her. Are you planning to go on another business trip?" Her sister was her usual unruffled self. "Or dare I hope that you're finally going to take a few days off for yourself?"

"Neither, I'm afraid." She kept her voice lightly regretful. "I've got some problems here at work that I need to concentrate on. Nothing crucial, but I'd feel a lot better if Merrie were in good hands the next few days."

"What's up, kiddo? I know you too well. You're upset about something." June's ready sympathy almost proved Cassie's undoing.

"I can't talk about it right now. Just trust me, sis. As soon as I can I'll come out and tell you about it, though whether I dare bring Merrie home or not—"

"Dare?" June echoed, outraged. "What's going on? Is Merrie in danger?"

"No, of course not. At least, I don't think so. Her—her father just showed up." She stumbled over the words.

"Bran Rathburne is here? In Bern?" June gasped. "What does he want? What are you going to do?"

"I don't know." Cassie's voice was weary. "I'm not even sure he knows who I am. But I want to keep Merrie as far out of his reach as possible until I find out what he wants."

"But what if he finds out about her? What if he shows up at my doorstep? How will I recognize him?" June worried.

"It'll be easy enough. Don't let anyone in who has Merrie's eyes. They're distinctive enough. But I don't think you have anything to worry about. He graduated from law school before he took over the Foundation. He's not going to do anything rash or foolish that might jeopardize his legal position."

"Maybe I should take her someplace. We could visit Cathy in Seattle...."

"And what would your three sons and your husband say to that?" Cassie replied reasonably. "I'm sure if we just sit tight, it'll work out. Either he's here by some ghastly coincidence and he'll be gone in a day or two, or he's here for some reason that he'll no doubt explain in his own sweet time. There's nothing we can do but keep calm." She took a deep, steadying breath, wishing she could follow her own good advice. "I can't thank you enough for taking care of Merrie for me. I don't know what I'd do without you. Give her a kiss for me and tell her Mama will be back soon." As she slowly, silently replaced the receiver she stared at it for a long pensive moment. Then, giving herself a little shake, she pushed back her tawny mane of hair, straightened her shoulders, and went back to join David and his businessmen. And Bran Rathburne.

Chapter Thirteen

"I can't imagine why you're so nervous, Sandra," David remarked casually, leaning past her to scoop a carrot stick through a huge dollop of sour cream dip. "You've done this sort of thing often enough before, and you do it so well. I guess we've taken advantage of you at Cooper, but you have such a flair for entertaining." He followed the carrot stick with a stalk of celery, adorned with at least two tablespoons of the fattening dip.

Despite her tension Cassie had to grin. "You can flatter me all you want, David. It has nothing to do with my supposed flair. It's because all you men are too lazy, or your wives know better. I'll have you know this is hardly the most enjoyable way to spend my birthday." She arranged glasses on the linen covered tray, casting a professional eye over the perfectly organized kitchen. The cocktail party for twenty-five people would practically run itself, she realized with a sigh of distant satisfaction. If only the rest of her life was so well organized.

"I realize that," he admitted, slightly abashed.
"And if you'd only mentioned it when I first proposed the idea, I never would have—"

"I thought it would be as good a way to spend the
time as any." She shrugged, taking pity on his guilt.
"It's not your fault that I changed my mind. I think I
would have been happier just spending the evening
alone with Merrie."

"Speaking of which, where is the little darling? I
thought she'd be having her dinner about now."

A stab of nervousness shot through Cassie as she
carried the tray out into the large wood-paneled living
room that was the center of the house. "I thought it
would be easier if she stayed with June," she replied
honestly. "And, David..."

"Hmmm?" He was into the quiche at this point.

"Would you do me a favor and not mention her to
any of the guests tonight?"

David's hazel eyes narrowed curiously behind his
thick glasses. "Any particular reason, Sandra?"

She shrugged again. "Not really," she lied. I just
prefer to keep my business private. I wouldn't want to
spend the evening talking about my daughter's prodi-
gious talents to someone like Margaret Graham or
Bran Rathburne." There, she congratulated herself.
That sounded neat and plausible.

"Rathburne, eh? Didn't he used to fund the Thompson Nutri-Center, where you and Alleyn worked?"
he questioned shrewdly, having been versed in the
sordid details of her professional, if not her personal,
history. "Do you know this guy?"

"I—I may have met him," she said vaguely. "I

don't really remember." Two could play at Bran's game, if game it was.

"Sandra, I find that extremely difficult to believe. With your powers of observation you're hardly likely to have forgotten meeting someone like Bran Rathburne. I may not be a female, but even I can see he's just the sort of man to appeal to a woman. All those dark, brooding good looks."

She met his curious gaze with all the firmness she could muster. "Well, if I did happen to meet him in the past, *he's* forgotten it, and I'd just as soon forget it, too." She untied her apron and tossed it back into the kitchen.

"Just as well," David mumbled, heading back toward the sour cream dip. "He's bringing his fiancée with him. At least I presume that's what she is—she's wearing the largest diamond I've ever seen outside a museum."

Cassie could only be glad that her back was turned. She hadn't thought it could hurt so much, she realized dispassionately. After all, it was to be expected. It was only surprising he wasn't already married.

"Fiancée?" she echoed casually, turning to face him with a brightly curious smile.

"Pretty little girl," David supplied. "Her name's Lucy something. I expect he'll be bringing her. She's really quite attractive. Speaking of attractive, did I tell you I like that dress? New, isn't it? And I like the way you've done your hair," he added naively.   .

"Yes, it's new," she admitted tonelessly. She had rushed out at lunchtime, scouring the shops for just the right thing to wear. Her motives were unclear, but the end result was anything but. The sea-foam green silk swirled gently around her riper curves, strained softly against her full breasts, and brought out green flecks in her honey-brown eyes. Her mother's diamonds dazzled in her ears, and her brown hair was pulled pack with an antique ivory comb. She look sophisticated, sensual, and very much in control of her life and herself. It was exactly the image she wanted to project. She alone knew that the image was hollow.

Every time the door opened that evening Cassie stiffened, determined not to turn and look. By the time the large living room was filled with chattering couples and the first arrivals were on their second round of drinks, she began to relax. He wasn't going to show up. He was just as horrified to see her as she had been to see him, and he had too much couth and grace to show up where he would so obviously be unwanted. No doubt he had bundled his fiancée and himself out of town on the first plane. His fiancée, she thought, her lip curling. Lucy Barrow, of all people. She thought he had better taste.

"What's the matter, Sandra?" David hovered near her, a smear of onion dip on his silk tie and his chin. "You look like you ate something nasty."

"You might say so," she said caustically, reaching up with a napkin and dabbing at his chin with maternal solicitude.

"I hope we're not too late." A familiar voice chose that moment to speak in her ear, and she stepped backward in sudden panic, treading on his foot and knocking into him.

Her face flamed as he righted her with the same

impersonal care he had exhibited earlier among the flower beds. The eyes that bore down into hers were still devoid of expression, the hand on her arm was light and noncommanding, and yet, Cassie was sure he knew her.

"I've never known you to be so clumsy, Sandra." David broke the silence with a cheerful laugh. "Old age must be getting to you."

"Old age?" Bran questioned lightly, his winged eyebrows raised inquiringly. "Surely you're not all that ancient, Miss Thayer. You couldn't be much older than thirty-five."

Once more David's boisterous laugh cut the tense stillness. "That's a good one. I bet you appreciate that, Sandra. She's thirty today, Bran, and you know as well as I do she hardly looks twenty-five. And you should call her Sandra. We're none of us very formal around here. Or if you must, make it *Ms.* Thayer. We've a liberated lady here."

"Ms. Thayer," he said, the lightly mocking emphasis carrying her back two years ago with a sudden, sickening whoosh. "May I wish you a happy birthday?" And before she could divine his intention he leaned down and caught her lips in a brief gentle kiss, his mouth warm and sweet against her astonished one.

It was the cruelest thing he could have done. Anger, passion, and contempt in a degradingly sensual kiss would have only served to ignite her anger. The soft, loving sweetness of his kiss mocked the hours they had spent in each others' arms and broke the last, tiny whole portion of her heart.

"Excuse me," she gasped, and dashed for the kitchen. It was thankfully deserted, and in the dim light she busied herself arranging more *crudité* on the pewter platter, her head bent to hid the glitter of angry tears in her eyes. In her headlong dash she had managed to catch a glimpse of Lucy Barrow, looking sleek and well fed and beautiful, like a Persian kitten, and the overlarge diamond ring had flashed mockingly at her as she made her escape.

"Are you all right, Sandra?" She hadn't heard David enter the room, but so gentle was his presence, she didn't even flinch.

"Fine, David," she replied, bending her head lower over the plate. "I just thought we needed some more carrots and celery."

"They've left."

At this point she raised her head to meet his too-understanding eyes. "Who's left?"

"Rathburne and his fiancée. He said to tell you he was sorry they had to run, but that he'd be seeing you soon, he hoped."

"That sounds like a threat," she said dully.

"I don't know whether he meant it that way. Do you want to talk about it, Sandra?"

She shook her head, the chestnut curtain swinging against her pale cheek. "Not now, David. But thank you."

"Think nothing of it. We won't mention it again until you want to talk about it. And we're having dinner tomorrow night, aren't we?"

Cassie looked up, startled. "I'd forgotten. I don't know, David. . . ."

"Best thing for you," he said firmly. "You promised you'd come—I have Helen as my witness."

She forced an unhappy little laugh. Tomorrow night
was the night she'd decided to sleep with dear, kind,
dependable David. But that was before Bran Rathburne had chosen such a diabolical moment to walk
back into her life. She knew now that she could no
sooner go to bed with David than she could seduce
old Dr. Gibson.

"Dinner would be very nice," she agreed. "But an
early one. I want to get home before it's too late."

"You have my word on it. Now, do you feel up to
rejoining your guests?" He held out his arm with
debonair politeness.

She took it, grateful for the sturdy feel of his arm
beneath her still-trembling fingers. "I do, indeed,"
she said, smiling at him bravely.

Despite Cassie's mounting dread, there was no sign of
Bran Rathburne or his fiancée anywhere near the
Cooper Laboratories the next day. His absence wasn't
enough to guarantee Cassie any peace of mind, however. At every moment she was expecting him to appear at her desk, or pop out from around a corner, so
that by lunchtime she was a nervous wreck. A hurried
visit to her sister's didn't prove much help—Merrie
was in the midst of a much-needed nap, and even
Cassie, who desperately needed to feel her child's
soft, cuddly little body in her arms, decided not to
wake her. She'd simply have to make it through the
next few days without her daughter. It felt as if her
one source of strength had been taken from her.

Dinner was a disaster. David, in a misguided effort to inject a note of celebration into the evening, chose the Coq d'Or for dinner, the most expensive and elegant restaurant in the small coastal city. It was also situated in the best hotel the town had to offer, so it should have come as no surprise to Cassie to see Bran and Lucy ushered to a table not far from theirs shortly after their cocktails were served.

Polite nods were exchanged from across the room, and Cassie swiftly drained the Scotch she had ordered to ward off the chilly rainy night. This was all she needed to cap her day, she thought. At least she had the dubious satisfaction of knowing that Lucy Barrow hadn't the faintest idea who she was. Of course, Lucy had only met her twice—once during that strange dinner party at Ellen's. The raucous female would have little resemblance to the quietly elegant Sandra Thayer—or so she hoped.

"Would you like to go somewhere else, Sandra?" David asked with his usual perceptive solicitude. "We don't have to stay here, you know."

Cassie shook her head vehemently. "I'm certainly not going to let him drive me away. We were here first, and I'm not about to move. I would, however, appreciate another drink. A double."

David's worried expression deepened, but he placed the order without comment, keeping up a steady stream of gentle, inconsequential chatter, to which Cassie replied with vague monosyllables as she toyed with her food. Her abstraction didn't seem to faze him, nor the frequent, furtive glances she sneaked toward Bran Rathburne and his fiancée. It was during the rich strawberry dessert that she didn't want that the slender jeweler's box appeared next to her third glass of whiskey.

"What's this?"

"Happy birthday, Sandra," David said softly, his eyes ardent in the candlelight. "I would have given this to you last night, but things were so hectic, I decided to wait for a quieter moment."

"David..." She hesitated, her slender ringless hand toying with the velvet box.

"Open it, Sandra," he pleaded softly, looking like an eager puppy. At that moment Cassie felt the familiar burning sensation at the back of her neck, and she didn't need to turn her head to know she suddenly had Bran's full attention. "Go ahead," David urged, and there was no way she could avoid it.

With nervous fingers she fumbled with the wrapping, then let out a reluctant gasp of admiration. Nestled in the satin lining was a whisper-thin gold chain, with a cloisonné pendant in the shape of a deep purple pansy at the end of it.

"Heartsease, Sandra," he said softly. "I know how much you love them, and I thought this would be a perfect remembrance of the first of what I hope will be many collaborations."

"Oh, David, it's absolutely lovely," she said simply.

He preened slightly, and with his blunt scientist's fingers lifted the delicate piece from its resting place. "May I?" At her shy nod he leaned across the table and fastened it around her neck. It lay against her lightly tanned skin, glowing above the simple clinging lines of the black silk dress that she hadn't worn for two years. What on earth had possessed her to wear it, tonight of all nights? she wondered. Unable to help herself, she turned in Bran's direction and then wished she hadn't. There was only one word for the expression in his silver-blue eyes as he stared at her, ignoring his fiancée, and that word was *murderous*.

Turning back to David, she slowly, deliberately leaned across the table and kissed him lightly on the lips. "Thank you, David," she murmured. "Thank you for everything." And her guilt was increased by the tender light in his eyes.

"I only wish you'd let me do more," he murmured shyly. "But as long as you know I'm always available..."

"I'll remember," she promised. Out of the corner of her eye she could see Bran hustling Lucy out of the restaurant. Fury seemed to vibrate through every inch of his tall frame, and Cassie noticed for the first time that he was thinner than he was two years ago. And surely there hadn't been all that silver in the curly black hair that framed his bleakly handsome face.

"Are you ready to leave, Sandra?" David was inquiring solicitously. "I know you wanted to make an early night of it."

"Let's wait just a bit more. I'd really rather not walk out with Mr. Rathburne and his fiancée."

"All right," he agreed, asking no questions with his usual tactful forbearance. "It's only half past seven — do you want to swing by your sister's and pick up Merrie on our way home?"

Cassie hesitated. "She's going to be staying with

June for another day or two," she said diffidently. "But I'd love to stop by and visit with her for a short while."

"No problem," he said solemnly. "Just let me take care of the check."

David's customary sensitivity extended even through the miserable ride home from June's. Merrie had been ecstatic to see her mother, clinging with a fierce possessiveness and shrieking with uncustomary temper when her aunt attempted to put her down for the night. The silver-blue eyes of her daughter looked up at her piteously, the chubby hands clung desperately, and for the first time Cassie began to see other resemblances. There was a look of Bran to her, even without the identical eyes. The silky black hair, the long limbs, the stubborn personality. As she was unable to tear herself away, Cassie held her baby until she fell sound asleep in her arms.

The first part of the drive out to Cassie's cliffside house was made in silence. It was Cassie who broke it, once she knew all danger of tears had passed. She hated to cry, particularly with an audience, even one as sympathetic as David.

"I don't suppose you have any idea how long Bran Rathburne is planning to stay in Oregon?" she said casually.

"It may be quite a while. Cooper Laboratories has applied for a substantial grant from the Rathburne Foundation. That's the reason he's here. They're very careful who they support, especially after the scandal at the Thompson Nutri-Center. I don't really expect he'll be leaving until he has a pretty thorough idea of our program," he said, his curiosity barely under control.

"Great," she said cynically.

"What's the problem, Sandra? Don't you like him? Has he been bothering you?"

"No, he hasn't been bothering me. Not in the way you mean. And no, I don't like him. He's arrogant, overbearing, and nosy. The less time I have to spend with him, the happier I'll be."

"He hasn't struck me as that sort," David said meditatively. "But I guess there's no accounting for personality differences. I don't know if you can manage to keep away from him. You're a key part of the Pharmacopoeia Project—he'll need to have some in-depth discussions with you as well as all the other assistant heads."

"I may have to take a leave of absence," she said wearily, the picture he conjured up chilling her.

"You can't, Sandra." His voice was sympathetic but adamant, and for the first time in a long while Cassie remembered that he wasn't simply her co-worker, he was her boss. "Without you, there'd be no Pharmacopoeia Project—at least not on its current scale." He sighed. "Dr. Gibson is very fond of you, but Cooper is his life. I don't think he'd forgive you if you let him down."

Slowly, carefully, Cassie digested that information. In the long run she didn't have much choice, she knew. Her daughter's well-being came before any mundane considerations such as her job, her career, or Cooper Laboratories. "I'll guess I'll have to cross that bridge when I come to it," she said evenly.

David pulled up at the bottom of the rock steps leading to her front door. "Would you rather go in by the garage? I can easily drive around back."

"No, this is fine." She jumped out of the stately Bonneville with unflattering haste. "You don't need to get out of the car, David."

"Of course I do," he replied ponderously, following her up the steps. "My mother taught me to always see a young lady to her door."

Cassie had left a light burning in her front hall. Before she could stop him, he'd followed her inside the door, his usual tact and sensitivity abandoning him for the moment.

Don't let him kiss me, she thought desperately.

But her wish went unanswered. Clumsily David pulled her slender body into his bearlike embrace, his mouth swooping down. As usual, in his excitement his aim was off somewhat, so that his closed-mouth kiss landed just below her nose. Quickly he compensated, pressing his tight lips grindingly against hers, and for one mischievous moment she wondered how shocked he'd be if she opened her mouth beneath his and sought his tongue. He'd probably faint dead away with horror, she realized with ill-placed amusement.

But it was her turn to be shocked as she felt an awkward hand reach up and clutch her breast in what he doubtless hoped was rough passion. It was closer to manhandling, and Cassie yanked herself abruptly out of his arms.

"David!" she said in shock.

He had the grace to look abashed. "I'm sorry, Sandra," he mumbled. "Tonight obviously isn't the night. It's just that... you're so beautiful in that black dress, and I've tried to be so patient. But I'm a man, after all.''

"You've been very patient," she soothed, taking his unresisting arm and leading him toward the door. "Please, David. Be patient just a little bit longer.''

"But I've been waiting for months!" he cried in frustration. "You know my intentions are honorable, Sandra. I want to marry you.''

"Please, David,'' she begged. "Not tonight.''

"Very well.'' There was just a trace of petulance in his usually kind voice. Leaning over, he kissed her briefly on the cheek. "I'll talk to you tomorrow.''

"Fine. Thank you again, David.'' She shut the door behind him with a sigh of relief, leaning her head against the paneling and shutting her eyes in exhaustion until she heard his car start up and drive away.

After turning off the outside light, she slipped off her shoes and padded barefoot into the dimly lit living room, stretching her arms over her head in a vain attempt to release the tension. It was the clink of ice that alerted her to his presence. She stood there, panicked and motionless as a trapped doe.

Slowly, elegantly, he rose from the upholstered chair, setting his glass down on a side table with a quiet snap. He was tall, dark, and dangerous in the muted light, and Cassie didn't know whether to run away from him or to him.

"He may have been waiting months, Cassie," he said in that husky voice that still had the power to mesmerize her. "But I've been waiting two years.'' And he started toward her.

Chapter Fourteen

In sudden panic she stumbled, knocking over a lamp in the process and stubbing her toe. Bran paused a moment in his headlong pursuit, a glint in his eye.

"You've gotten a lot clumsier in the last two years," he observed meditatively. "You never used to fall over things. Or do I make you nervous?"

Somewhere she found her voice. "I would say that's a distinct possibility. What are you doing here, Bran?" As she set the heavy lamp upright she turned it on, sending a small pool of light into the room, banishing a part of the dangerous darkness. It only brought Bran's overwhelming presence into clearer focus.

He had changed. There were more lines around his eyes, and a leaner, more finely honed look to his strong body. He had changed from the dark, almost somber suit he'd worn at dinner to a pair of faded jeans that hugged his lean hips and long legs, and his blue chambray shirt was unbuttoned partway down to expose a tanned chest with a fine mat of dark hair.

Cassie remembered the feel of that hair-roughened chest pressing down against her soft breasts, and she remembered it far too well. She took an involuntary step back. If anything, the years had made him even more dangerously attractive, though she would never have thought it possible.

"You really are frightened of me?" The idea seemed to bring him some sort of cool amusement, a fact that failed to comfort Cassie. "What took you so long to get home? I've been here for over an hour. I was getting ready to drive over to Tremayne's apartment and beat his door down."

"What business is it of yours where I was?" she shot back bravely. "And how did you get in here? I left the place locked."

Her anger left him completely unmoved. "You should never underestimate me, Cassie. You did two years ago, and it was a great mistake. Why did you leave?" The question was barked out abruptly.

"I would think that was obvious," she replied with a fair attempt at bravery. "You told me quite clearly that you neither liked nor trusted me. I suppose I should have been grateful that you were willing to sleep with me despite your reservations, but then, I was never the humbly grateful type."

She had succeeded in ruffling that almost detached calm of his. "Damn it, you never even left me a note. Not a word, not a phone call. Meredith was frantic, certain I'd driven you away."

"I did call."

"She was ready to—What?" Her words penetrated his abstraction.

"I said I did call," she repeated patiently. "Almost a year after I left I called you, late one evening. Your fiancée answered the phone."

He didn't even have the grace to look abashed. "I never got the message. You did leave a message, didn't you?"

Raising her chin, she looked him straight in the eyes. "I hung up on her."

The beginnings of a smile tugged at one corner of his mouth. "Why? Were you jealous?"

"Not after that long," she said loftily.

"Then why did you call me?"

She was getting on dangerous ground with this. Immediately she changed tack. "You still haven't told me what you're doing here."

The smile widened, a shark's smile, one that she didn't trust for a moment. "I would have thought that would be obvious. I wanted to see you—see how you were doing in your new life here. It took a private investigator exactly two hours to determine your whereabouts." He leaned forward, and Cassie could feel his body heat, smell the achingly familiar scent of his spicy after-shave. "What were you trying to hide from, Cassie, that you made such a clumsy attempt at covering your tracks? Were you afraid I was going to drag you back like some outraged caveman?" His voice was icy cold and cruel. "I'm not an obtuse man, Cassie. You made it perfectly clear that you wanted nothing more to do with me. I wasn't about to chase after you."

"I couldn't take the chance," she mumbled, thinking her heart should be inured to pain by now. Why did his cold contempt cut into her like a knife? she wondered.

"There are a great many other willing women, Cassie," he said in that gentle, wicked voice.

"I'm sure there are. In which case, why are you here now?"

Bran took another step, one that brought him within reach of her. Resolutely she stood her ground. "I was curious. Meredith just had her first child. They named her Cassandra. It brought you to mind."

A fresh wave of pain washed over her. She stared at him, aching, but fortunately he expected no response. "She wants you to be godmother. She'd like you to come east for the christening."

"That's impossible," she stammered, her mouth dry.

He nodded. "I told her you'd say that. After all, you're such a consummate coward—always running away instead of facing a problem and trying to work it out." One strong tanned hand reached out and brushed the curtain of sun-streaked hair from her face. She flinched, and an unreadable expression darkened his eyes.

"Well, for once you were right about me," she managed, trying hard not to jerk away from that slightly callused hand. "So now that you've satisfied your curiosity, why don't you go away? Go back to Virginia, and give Meredith and Mrs. Bellingson my love."

"Mrs. Bellingson retired shortly after you left. She didn't approve of the way I treated you. I tried to explain that I was an innocent party, but she'd have none of it. She told me she wouldn't come back until you did." His hand moved down to lightly graze the side of her neck. She shivered slightly, trying to control her reaction to his nearness. "And I haven't quite satisfied my curiosity about you. There was one more thing I wanted to check." His voice was low, husky, and unbearably beguiling. Cassie felt a fire begin to blaze within her, and her knees weakened.

"What was that?" Her voice came out as little more than a whisper as she felt herself being mesmerized by the glow in his eyes.

"I wanted to find out if you still wanted me as much as I want you," he whispered, his hand slipping behind her neck and drawing her, with agonizing deliberation, to him.

She had plenty of time to pull away, to shake off his warm grip. With a small helpless sigh she shut her eyes as she felt her soft breasts press up against the solid wall of his chest. His lips met hers, warm and sweet and surprisingly tentative, lightly brushing the trembling contours of her mouth. As his mouth continued its slow, incredibly erotic dance of desire, his hips pressed against hers, and she felt his heated longing with distant surprise. All the time he'd been saying such cruel, hurtful things he'd been wanting her, needing her.

His mouth abandoned hers for a moment, and she could feel his eyes boring down into hers. "Do you still want me?" he queried softly.

She shook her head, determined to resist the irresistible. "No," she whispered, her arms still at her sides.

Once more his mouth caught hers. This was no gentle exploration, this was passionate demand. Catching her wrists, he pulled her arms around his lean waist, pulled her closer into the powerful warmth of his body. Cassie felt her last, tenuous control slip and dissolve beneath the powerful thrust of his warm sweet tongue, and shyly, boldly, she met his advance. She could hear him moan deep in the back of his throat, and the sound excited her as nothing else had. Pressing her advantage, she banished the last tiny shred of wisdom and judgment, reveling in the feel of his body pressed against hers. This was where she had longed to be, ached to be, for the past two years. Surely this one night could be allowed her by that turncoat fate that had alternately smiled and frowned on her. Surely she could have just this one night, she reasoned.

His mouth scattered soft hungry kisses across her cheekbone, his tongue tracing the delicate lines of one small ear beneath the thick chestnut hair. "You do want me as much as I want you." There was a ragged note of triumph in his voice.

"No." She sighed. He pulled away, looking down into her upturned face and cradling her neck with his long fingers.

"No?" he echoed, disbelieving.

"No," she said. "I want you more."

Bran stared down at her for a long unbelieving moment. "Impossible," he said softly, a crooked tender smile lighting his dark face.

His mouth caught hers once more, and it was as if her words had unleashed a raging torrent within both of them. Suddenly she couldn't have enough of him. Her eager hands ripped open the buttons on his shirt, sliding inside against the warm skin that ignited her desires even further. She was trembling all over in the demanding shelter of his arms, her mouth and tongue answering his in their unspoken language. Deft hands, wise from memory, untied the front wrap of her black dress, and a moment later it dropped to the floor, leaving her clad in nothing but a thin wisp of rose silk panties. With a muffled groan he sank to his knees in front of her, his mouth worshiping the softly rounded warmth of her belly, his tongue dipping lightly into her navel.

Cassie drew him to her, pressing his head against the soft swell of her breasts. With gentle deftness he pulled her down, until she was lying stretched out on the thick soft carpet, her hair a halo behind her head.

His eyes never left hers as he shed his clothes quickly and gracefully, then eased her panties off her hips with gentle hands. And then his eyes narrowed as they fell on the new pendant lying between her breasts. Before she could guess his intention he had reached out and yanked it off her, throwing it across the room.

"Don't wear that again," he ordered harshly, his voice and face full of a savage possessiveness that both aroused and angered her.

"Show me why," she challenged him.

And he proceeded to do so, filling her with his massive strength until she wept with the joy of it. They made love with fierce, rapid passion, desperate for the feel of each other. Her hands slid over his smoothly muscled back, and then her nails dug in as her world burst into a shower of stars, and Bran followed, his voice hoarse in her ear as he called her name, over and over again, before collapsing, spent, in her welcoming arms.

After a long time, when their heartbeats had slowed and their breathing returned to normal, he lifted his head and looked down into her eyes. If she hadn't known better, she would have thought there were tears glittering in his eyes. But she knew that was impossible.

"Why did you run away?" His voice was soft, gentle, and for the life of her, Cassie couldn't remember what foolish pride had made her leave the heaven of his arms.

She reached up a gentle hand, brushing the tumbled black hair back from his high forehead. "I had to," she whispered, certain at least of that.

"No, you didn't," he contradicted flatly, his swift bruising kiss lessening the severity somewhat. And then the kiss slowed, deepened into something else, and only the need for breath forced him to break away. "Where's your bedroom?" he demanded huskily.

She was still breathless from the sudden, overwhelming return of passion. "First door on the left."

Without another word he scooped her up in his arms, carrying her across the living room to the large bedroom with its balcony overlooking the sea. Carefully he laid her down on her wide lonely bed, stretching out beside her, his eyes never leaving her face. "I'm spending the night," he said softly, a tender hand stroking the side of her flushed face. "Any objections?"

"Would it do me any good?" she countered, feeling strangely docile.

"Not a bit." His head dropped down, his mouth capturing one rosy-tipped breast with a slow, teasing motion.

"Then I won't even try."

Chapter Fifteen

Slowly, Cassie edged her body away from Bran's sleeping form, sliding delicately out of his grasp. In his sleep he reached out for her, his arms falling away when they encountered only empty space where she had been.

Pausing by the bed for a moment, she stared down at him in the predawn light, just as she had two years ago, moments before she left him. Not that the situation had improved. There were still irreconcilable problems between them: lack of trust, respect, tenderness. Although how could she feel that after the exquisite tenderness of his lovemaking last night? But that tenderness didn't seem to survive long out of bed.

She pulled her navy velour bathrobe around her and padded toward the bathroom, closing the bedroom door silently on its sleeping occupant. As she headed down the hallway her daughter's doorway stood as a mute reproach to her and the reluctantly healthy glow in her tired, aching body. How could she have fallen under his spell again, even for a moment?

How could she have let her guard down, when her daughter's safety and well-being depended on her? she chastised herself.

Opening the door, she allowed her eyes to wander about the lonely expanse of the pretty little nursery, to the empty crib, the stack of clean diapers, and the toys, in perfect order. Reaching behind the doorknob, she turned the lock before shutting the door with a silent, final click. She had no key for the lock, but that was a problem she could deal with later, after Bran had left her to deal with her guilt and recriminations.

Cassie turned the shower on full, as hot as she could bear it, and stood under the punishing stream, hoping for some sort of comfort or common sense to come to her. But there was nothing but cleanliness awaiting her in the shower. She could wash away the scent of him from her body, but she couldn't wash away the feel of his hands on her flesh, or the tiny bruise marks he'd inadvertently left. He was in her blood and in her body, and not even the Pacific Ocean could wash him away. Only time and distance, which had made a fair start on it, could accomplish that.

The early morning light flooded the kitchen as she made a pot of strong black coffee, knowing Bran would want some eventually, knowing she had to at least offer him that much before she did her best to drive him away.

She didn't dare try to retrieve her clothes from the bedroom. Her resolve hadn't hardened sufficiently. All he had to do was open up those magnificent eyes of his and stretch out his arms and she would throw caution to the winds—and that was the one thing she couldn't afford to do.

Still dressed in her enveloping velour robe, she took a huge mug of the strong steaming black coffee and stepped out onto the window-tossed balcony that overlooked the angry Pacific. The wind was warmer this morning, and as she stretched out on the redwood chaise she took the first sip of coffee, letting out a small weary sigh. The sunlight was bright and strong in the early morning hours, strong enough to dry her shower-damp hair in record time, she thought. It caught the rain-drenched rocks beneath her, sparkled on the wind-tossed trees, bejeweled the tiny flowers that grew along the winding drive to the side of the house. Why did they always make love in the rain? Cassie wondered wearily. It must be a sign of some sort—fate trying to tell her that they were doomed. And this time she would listen, she told herself. Last night would never happen again—not if she could help it. There was too much at stake, not the least of which was her newfound peace of mind and her daughter's security. Firmly she pushed that old, familiar guilt away as she closed her eyes to the bright sunlight. Eventually, after Bran was long gone back to Virginia and married to vapid little Lucy and had children of his own, then she might tell him. But he already had a child of his own, her mind argued fairly. And he had a right to know. But not yet, she decided.

The soft sea-tangled breeze ruffled her damp hair around her face, its usual soothing effect blunted by the emotion of the night she had just shared. It was with a curious clutching at her heart that she realized what hurt the most. It was not the moments of passion, sublime and transcendent as they were, but after they had made love the second time, in the warm soft cocoon of her celibate bed, after she'd moved away and withdrawn into herself, he'd pulled her back into his arms, cradling her head against his neck, holding her with an intense longing that had unleashed the dam of tears that she'd held back for so long. And it was the desperate intensity of that embrace that haunted her now, as she set the coffee mug back on the deck and closed her eyes to the bright May sunshine, and would probably haunt her until the day she died.

It started as a faint tickling across her cheekbones. As she opened her eyes she came face to face with Bran's blue-eyed gaze. His hair had tickled her skin, the black curls still damp from a shower. As her eyes widened she took in the full glory of him. He was clad only in his faded denims of the night before, and droplets of water still beaded the mat of hair on his broad tanned chest. He was squatting down beside her, one hand trailing gentle fingers across her lips, her eyelids, her nose, and then he levered forward, and his lips followed his fingertips, ending with a gentle kiss on her trembling lips. And she was too bemused to stop him, her mouth opening beneath his gently probing one, willingly deepening the kiss into one of slow, drugged passion.

Reluctantly he pulled away, his smile a flash of white in his dark face. "That's enough of that, woman," he warned with mock severity. "I need my coffee before anything else in the morning."

"Before anything?" she echoed innocently. The velour robe had somehow become parted, exposing one long tanned leg and a great deal of creamy smooth breast.

"Before anything," he verified, reaching out and pulling her robe closed with hasty hands.

She smiled with a trace of triumph. "The coffee's on the stove," she said, not moving. "It won't take but a minute to heat it."

If he was taken aback by her refusal to wait on him, he didn't show it. "Do you want some more?" He picked up her half-empty mug, the coffee now cold.

"Please." It was a small word, but it brought flooding back the memories of last night to both of them, when her "please" had been begging for something quite different. She could feel a blush suffuse her face at his slow sexy smile.

"My pleasure," he said softly, disappearing into the house on silent bare feet. Cassie watched his tall straight back vanish into the kitchen, and that clutching feeling in her heart tightened. Why did he have to be so beautiful? And why did she, after all these years, still love him, love him so much that any other man, including a sweet, devoted, attractive man like David Tremayne, left her unmoved?

Lost in abstraction, she hadn't noticed his return until a brown well-shaped hand held her refilled mug beneath her nose. Reaching up to take it, she tried to avoid touching him. Deliberately his fingers grasped hers as he handed her the coffee so that the two of them held it for a long silent moment. And then he released her, moving back to perch on the railing, taking a long gulp of his own coffee.

"What's behind the locked door, Cassie?" he inquired curiously.

It took all her control not to choke on the sip of coffee she'd just taken. Everything depended on how she handled this, she knew. Bran wasn't a man to be easily fooled.

"Storage," she said calmly enough. "And what makes you think you have any right to go ferreting through my house?"

A shadow darkened the concerned angles of his face, and the curious expression was masked by a cool bland one. "I was looking for the bathroom," he explained curtly. "One door led to a linen closet, one door was locked. The third door I struck it lucky. So what's the locked door all about? Bluebeard's chamber?"

He couldn't leave it alone, could he, she thought miserably. Part of her had vainly hoped they could part on amiable terms, that some of the gentleness and understanding of the night before could remain, to comfort her on the long, lonely nights ahead. Apparently, that wasn't to be. She had to protect her daughter, first and foremost, and the wickedly handsome man sitting so arrogantly on her front balcony, as if he belonged there, posed a very real threat to their comfortable way of life.

"None of your business." She didn't notice the coffee sloshing as she set it down sharply on the deck beside her. *Watch it, Cassie,* she warned herself hastily. *If you're too secretive, he'll never give up until he finds out what you're hiding.* "It's my office," she said in a calmer tone of voice. "I keep my records in there, and a small lab setup, and my notes. I don't like strangers pawing through them."

A winged eyebrow rose mockingly, in silent acceptance of the battle lines once more drawn. "Strangers?" he queried. "You have a long line of them tramping through your house?"

Cassie couldn't resist. "I locked it this morning."

There was no mistaking the withdrawal on his face. But was there hurt in his eyes? Cassie hadn't been used to considering Bran as in any way vulnerable, capable of being hurt. Before she could open her mouth to call back the callous words, he rose to his full height, stretching with a lazy grace that nevertheless couldn't disguise the tension in every muscle of his beautiful body.

"I would say you've made yourself perfectly clear." His voice was its usual low husky drawl. "I can let myself out." Taking his empty coffee mug and hers, he moved back into the house. Cassie sat there, torn by indecision, until he reappeared a few minutes later, his chambray shirt unbuttoned with the shirttails loose around his lean hips and his tennis shoes in one hand. He stood looking down at her, his expression shuttered. And then he allowed the confusion to surface as he squatted down beside her still figure, one hand reaching out to catch her cold limp one.

"I don't have to leave, you know," he said softly, his thumb gently stroking her palm.

Reluctantly she pulled herself out of the dazed torpor of pain. "I think it would be better if you did," she said with great calm.

The word he uttered then was short, sharp, and obscene, and he let go of her hand to stand up, anger and bewilderment written in his tall lean frame. "All right, if that's what you want."

"That's what I want," she said dully.

He let out an exasperated breath. "Then I'll go. But we're going to have to talk sometime, you know. We can't just leave it like this."

"Why not? You have to get back to Virginia before long. I'm sure this is very boring for Lucy. And I have my own life to live." It all sounded so calm and practical. "Last night was...pleasant, for old times' sake, you could say. But we can hardly make a habit of it. You have Lucy, and I have various...other...obligations."

"Such as David Tremayne?" Jealousy was rich in his voice. "And are your nights with him equally... pleasant? No, don't bother to answer that."

"I have no intention of doing so." She rose to her feet, fluidly, gracefully, her thick chestnut hair a wind-tossed curtain against her pale face. The smell of the rain-damp grass was strong in her nostrils, assailing her senses, as she faced her lover with calm pride. "I think it would be better if we didn't see each other again."

Bran watched her for a long silent moment, but Cassie kept her composure. "I'm sure you think that," he said finally, his voice heavy. "But that's not the way it's going to be. I'll give you time, since you seem to need it, but we're going to talk, sooner or later."

"No." She shook her head stubbornly.

"Yes," he said gently, inexorably. And before she could divine his intention his hand slid behind her neck, under her thick hair, and drew her face up to his. His kiss was swift and deep and angry, and when he released her, she was trembling with the completeness of it. "See you."

And then he was gone, out of her house, out of her life, most likely. She could hear the front door slam with heavy finality. A quiet moan of pain escaped her as she crawled back onto the chaise. After pulling her knees up to her chin, she stared sightlessly out at the angry ocean.

Chapter Sixteen

"Sandra!" David's gentle voice came from directly behind her, and she started nervously. "Sorry, didn't mean to make you jump. You've been incredibly edgy this last week."

"Have I?" she said, pushing a hand through her mane of hair. "I hadn't realized that I was any more nervous than usual."

"Don't be ridiculous, you're usually one of the most restful people I know."

"I suppose it's just missing Merrie." Cassie sighed, leaning against one apricot-painted wall. Dr. Gibson had insisted the hallways of Cooper Laboratories be painted pleasing colors, and Cassie herself had chosen this particular shade. Usually it soothed her, but this past week she'd been beyond soothing.

"Is she still with June?" David queried, startled. "I would have thought you'd brought her home days ago."

"I would have, but I'm so distracted with this funding business..." she said vaguely, averting her gaze from his observant eyes. "Every time I turn around I have some meeting to go to. I can't give her the attention she needs right now, and June's there..." She let it trail, knowing how lame it sounded. But she certainly wasn't going to give David any more information than she had to. "And, please, David, I'd rather not talk about her. You know I like to keep my personal life separate from my work."

"No, I didn't know that," he said dryly. "I've noticed that Merrie's picture has disappeared from your desk, and that every time anyone asks you about your daughter, you turn pale and look around to see if Bran Rathburne is anywhere in hearing distance." Taking her arm, he led her into the spacious confines of her office, shutting the door behind them. "I'm not unobservant, Sandra. It's easy to see what's behind all this mysterious behavior of yours."

"It is?" she questioned warily, her honey-brown eyes guarded.

"Of course." His usually gentle voice was patient and understanding, devoid of the latent flirtatiousness that had begun to creep into their daily conversations in the last few months. "You're in love with him, aren't you?"

"With Bran Rathburne?" Cassie managed a creditable laugh. "Don't be ridiculous."

"It's not ridiculous, it's more than obvious," he said sadly. "And it's obvious you're afraid he's going to find out about Merrie. He doesn't even know she exists. We were discussing you yesterday, and it became quite clear that he hasn't the faintest idea you're a mother."

"Discussing me? Why were you doing that?" She was incensed.

"Sandra, we were discussing all the researchers crucial to the Pharmacopoeia Project. And I thought it surprising, given the interest he's shown in you over the last week since he's been here, that he wouldn't know about Merrie—that her name wouldn't have come up in conversation."

"And what did you deduce from that?" she asked, her mouth dry.

"That you're afraid he'd lose interest in you if he found you came equipped with a ready-made family," David said smugly, pleased with his deductive reasoning.

Cassie swallowed a sigh of relief. "What makes you think he has any interest in me in the first place?"

David shook his sandy head. "I've seen the way he looks at you, seen the way you sneak looks at him when you think no one can see you. And I've watched you duck every single time he's wanted to meet with you, always finding some excuse."

"And that's love?" Her voice was caustic.

"Or something pretty close to it," he agreed smugly.

Cassie took a deep breath. "You can believe that all you want. Though I don't think it reflects very well on your opinion of me, to think I'd bundle Merrie off because I was afraid some arrogant, obnoxious, overbearing man might find her an inconvenience—"

"I wouldn't have called Rathburne obnoxious or overbearing. He can be a bit arrogant, especially if he's convinced he's right, but I can't really fault him for that. I like a man who fights for what he believes in."

"Hmmph. The sooner he leaves Oregon, the happier I'll be. Believe me."

A sad smile lit his eyes behind the horn-rimmed glasses. "You'd better convince yourself. You'll have plenty of time to do that. He's leaving in two or three days."

Cassie told herself that was relief flooding through her. "Is he? I would have thought he'd be gone long ago."

"I think he rather likes our part of the country," David said naively.

"Good. Let him enjoy it in Washington or northern California. I—" The shrill ringing of her telephone cut her off in midsentence, and with uncustomary shortness she grabbed the receiver and barked into it. "Yes?"

"Ms. Thayer? This is Lucy Barrow." The light affected voice hadn't changed in the two years since Cassie had heard it. No, it had been only thirteen months, the night she'd tried to tell Bran about his daughter.

Deliberately she put on her most businesslike tone. "How can I help you, Miss Barrow? I haven't seen your fiancé today, but perhaps Dr. Tremayne might be able to help you."

"Actually, I wanted to see you, Ms. Thayer. I wondered, could we meet for lunch?" The voice was guileless, but Cassie knew better. All her suspicions were instantly aroused.

"I don't think I could possibly—"

"This is my last day here, Ms. Thayer. I'm going back to Virginia this evening, but I think it's terribly important that we have a chance to talk. For old times' sake." There was just a trace of a sly threat in that voice, Cassie noted absently.

She hesitated for a moment longer, then gave in. If Lucy Barrow was so threatened by her that she was forcing a no-doubt unpleasant meeting, it was the least Cassie could do to reassure her that she had no interest in, no claim on, Bran Rathburne. "Where shall we meet?" she said finally.

Lucy quickly named a small dark restaurant halfway across town, a place where no one would be likely to see them. So that's the way it was going to be, Cassie thought.

"I couldn't possibly get away before two o'clock." She stalled for time.

"Two o'clock will be fine. And, Ms. Thayer... there's no need to mention this to anyone."

"I had no intention of doing so, Miss Barrow," she said coolly, placing the receiver down gently and meeting David's quizzical expression.

"What did she want? Rathburne's been trying to send her back to Virginia for days now, but she was having none of it. What's she want with you?"

"Well, apparently he's managed to persuade her to go. She's leaving tonight but wants to have lunch with me before she departs."

"Warning you off, eh?" David said appreciatively. "She knows a threat when she sees one."

"Hardly, David."

"Then why would she want to meet with you? She

hasn't shown any interest in anyone other than her precious fiancé during .the entire time she's been here, as far as I can see. She's heartily bored by the whole of Cooper Laboratories and the Pharmacopoeia Project in particular. If you ask me, I think there's trouble in paradise. I think Rathburne wants to do more than just get her out of the state. He has the look of a man who knows he's made a bad mistake and is hoping it's not too late to remedy it."

"Damn it, I didn't ask you!" Cassie snapped, unable to help herself. Immediately she regretted it. "I'm sorry, David. I didn't mean to yell at you. I'm just tired of the chaos Rathburne and his possible grant are causing in our lives. I just want things to get back to normal."

"I doubt if they're ever going to, old girl," he said sadly, heading for the door. "Enjoy your lunch."

As Cassie threaded her way between the closely set tables at Antonio's, she could feel the tension stretched taut inside her. One small boon was granted to her—the place was almost deserted at that late hour. There was only the elegant blonde who awaited her. In Cassie's nervous state she hadn't needed running into Bran on her way out to lunch. She had been rushing around the corner, late as usual, when a sixth sense warned her whom she might meet. She stopped short, coming face to face with him.

He looked tired, and his eyes were brooding in his tanned face. Looking down at her flustered face from his superior height, a slightly mocking smile had tugged at his mobile mouth.

"In a hurry, Cassie?" he inquired in that low husky drawl that melted her nerve ends.

"Yes, I am," she said briskly, moving past him. A strong hand had shot out, catching her arm in an iron grip that refused denial.

"We still haven't had that talk. You've done a magnificent job of avoiding me. If you're even half as efficient in your work, the Rathburne Foundation will be more than happy."

"Let go of my arm," she said in a low warning voice. "People will see us."

His smile widened, the mockery changing into almost hurt bitterness. "And we wouldn't want people to talk, would we, Cassie?"

"I certainly would think you wouldn't want them to," she stated quite calmly. "After all, you have a fiancée and a reputation to consider. I have neither." It was her first direct reference to the Stanley Alleyn affair, and Bran had the grace to wince.

"Things are not always as they seem," he said slowly. "I wouldn't believe everything people told you, if I were you."

"Why not? You did." And with that she yanked her arm from his grasp and practically ran out of the building.

But now, as Lucy Barrow looked up from the menu, a smug expression on her pretty, childish face, Cassie wished more than anything that she'd headed straight home. Bran and his fiancée were more than she felt able to cope with right now. Only two more days, David had said. In two days they'd both be gone, and she could have her baby back, and life

could resume its normal placid course, as if the events
of this week hadn't happened. And what was she doing, still believing in fairy tales? Her life would never
be the same.

"Miss Barrow?" She greeted the woman as she
took her place in the seat opposite her.

"Thank you for coming, Ms. Thayer. Or should I
say Ms. O'Neill?" The gloves were off, and by the
malicious light in her opponent's eye, Cassie could
tell Lucy was prepared to enjoy herself. "I've taken
the liberty of ordering for both of us. I know you'll
have to return to work before long."

Cassie eyed her warily. "That's very kind of you,
Lucy. And kind of you to remember me after so
long."

"Oh, I remember you very well," she assured her
sweetly. "You made quite an indelible impression at
Ellen's party that night. And then, of course, Bran's
reaction to your departure would hardly be termed as
mild. Of course, I'm not complaining. I reaped the
benefits of your desertion."

"I wouldn't have termed it desertion." Cassie
reached for the glass of strong red wine in front of her
and took a deep swallow. "And I wouldn't have
thought he'd have noticed I was gone."

"Oh, he noticed, all right. One more betrayal by the
female species. You see, I understand him very well. I
know my aunt Ellen had a less than desirable influence on him. And no one else seemed able to get
close to him. You had me worried for a bit, though.
He took you a great deal more seriously than he had
ever taken a female before. But then you took off,

when Meredith was barely out of danger, and Bran decided you were just like everyone else. And then he turned his attention back to me. Oh, he went through a few brief, furious affairs first, trying, I suppose, to drive you out of his system, but then he noticed I was still around, waiting patiently for him to come to his senses. And he turned to me, as I knew he would." She turned her hand so that the gaudy bright yellow diamond shone in the dimly lit restaurant. "A man doesn't give a ring like this without it meaning something."

Cassie leaned back, feigning a calm she was far from feeling. "Depends on the man," she drawled casually. "If I was presented with something like that, I might feel I was being paid for my favors."

The beautiful blue eyes opposite Cassie's narrowed for a moment, and the lips curled in a half snarl, half smile. "Perhaps that's the way men treat you, dear," she cooed kindly. "Bran and I understand each other."

"I'm so glad." A huge plate of steaming pasta was placed in front of her. Cassie was barely able to restrain a shudder, her stomach tied in tiny knots. Resolutely she took up a fork, determined not to let the nasty child-woman across from her know how deeply she rattled her. "You might answer a question for me, Lucy. Did you know Bran was coming to see me when you left Virginia?" She swallowed her first bite of pasta with difficulty.

"Of course I knew." Lucy threw back her blond mane with a carefully practiced gesture. "He made it very clear. We were about to set the date for our wedding, and he felt he had to make sure to tie up any loose ends, emotionally speaking. I'm a very understanding woman, so I agreed to accompany him."

"He told you that?" Cassie was obviously skeptical.

"Not in so many words. We have no need to be quite so blunt. But it was more than clear to me, and that's why I'm leaving ahead of him. I thought a few days more around you, and he'll be cured for good."

"And how do you expect that to happen?" Cassie pushed her plate away from her and reached for the wine. "If he isn't cured yet, why should you suppose I'll drive him away in the next two days?"

A small merciless smile of triumph lit her companion's face, and quite dispassionately Cassie could see why Bran would be in love with her. Lucy was quite breathtakingly beautiful.

"Oh, various reasons," Lucy said lightly. "For one thing, you want to drive him away. You don't want him here any more than I do."

"True enough," Cassie conceded, wondering what was coming next.

"And I think that once he finds out you bore him a daughter and never told him, he'll be so disgusted and furious with you that he'll never want to see you again."

The wineglass in Cassie's hand spilled, the dark red wine spreading across the tablecloth toward her companion like a bloodstain, the slightly sour odor mixing with the garlic and spices from the plate in front of her. "What are you talking about?" She made no effort to sop up the mess, just stared at the petite figure across from her, like a mother bear determined to defend her cub.

"I know all about Merrie," she said smugly.

"How?" The word was terse.

She smiled, that self-satisfied smirk that enraged Cassie. "Oh, I have my ways," she said airily. "Did you know that Bran hired a private investigator to find you?"

"I knew that," Cassie said grimly.

"Did you? I wonder how? But that's neither here nor there. Once Bran was finished with him, I hired him myself, to fill in the details. And I was fascinated to find out you'd had a child almost nine months to the day that you left Virginia. A daughter named Meredith."

"And I can assume you told Bran your exciting little news?"

The thick eyelashes batted down over the limpid blue eyes. "Of course I didn't. It's much more effective this way. If I told him, he'd be furious, but he'd be furious at me, too. As it is, he's bound to find out sooner or later. It's only been sheer luck that someone hasn't said anything yet. But I'd just as soon have you sweat it out. And who knows, he may never find out. If he follows me home in two days, it will mean he's finally lost interest in you, and your little secret is safe. If, however, he pursues the matter, you won't be able to hide your bastard's existence much longer, will you? And then—" She broke off, gasping, as Cassie threw the full contents of her water glass in her adversary's face.

With great calm and grace Cassie rose, grabbed her purse, and took two steps away. Then, thinking better of it, she turned back, picked up her plate of pasta, and dumped it in Lucy's lap.

"Thank you for lunch," she said politely, and strolled from the restaurant.

Chapter Seventeen

Cassie's elation lasted for a half hour at the most, and then panic set in. The very thought that Lucy Barrow held such crucial information in her slender little hands was terrifying, and to have gone so far as to toss a plate of pasta in her lap—satisfying though it had been—was practically suicidal. The only thing that stood between Bran's finding out about Merrie and safety was Lucy's goodwill. Cassie had to admit there was a good chance she'd forfeited any claim to Lucy's beneficence.

Nevertheless, Lucy might still keep her mouth shut. It all depended, doubtless, on how she thought the situtation would most benefit her. Cassie could only cross her fingers and pray.

She was far too wrought up to go back to work that afternoon. Instead she drove straight to her sister's house, fetching a delighted Merrie and taking her for a long drive up the coast. They stopped for an early supper at a fast-food restaurant, Merrie having recently discovered the intricate art of dipping French fries into ketchup, and then drove on up toward the north. It was dark when Cassie finally admitted that they had to turn back. She couldn't just disappear, take Merrie and run, much as she longed to. With her daughter sleeping soundly in her sturdy car seat, Cassie drove through the night, back to Bern and her sister's house to drop Merrie off again, with a set expression on her face, tears in her honey-brown eyes, and panic in her heart.

Her own house was silent and dark as she let herself in sometime after midnight. Never had Cassie felt so alone. She barely had the energy to stand under the cool stream of the shower before stumbling into the bedroom, dressed in her customary sleeping attire of an over-size T-shirt that had once, two years ago, belonged to Bran.

Her queen-size bed lay stretched out before her, cold and empty and so very lonely. With a small sad curse Cassie reached out and grabbed one of the soft feather pillows, yanked the thick comforter that covered the neatly made expanse of bed, and stalked back into the living room. She wouldn't spend one more sleepless night in that damn bed, reaching for someone who wasn't there and never would be again, she determined.

After tossing the pillow down on the sofa, she wrapped the voluminous folds of the quilt around her slender body and curled up on the couch in a tight miserable ball, prepared for another sleepless night.

The next thing she knew, strong sunlight was blazing into her eyes, and then just as suddenly was blocked out, as Bran moved in front of her.

Cassie was instantly alert, the last traces of drowsiness disappearing. "How did you get in here?" she demanded hoarsely.

"The same way I got in here last time," he replied calmly, lowering his long lean body into the armchair beside her makeshift bed. "You keep forgetting to lock the basement door."

"I won't again," she snapped, eyeing him warily. Had Lucy told him? she wondered.

A cool smile lit Bran's face. "I'll find another way in," he promised. "Do you always sleep so late?"

"On my day off I do."

"And why have you taken to sleeping on the couch? Does your bed suddenly make you uncomfortable? It is a bit big for one person."

"It has unpleasant memories," she shot back, and he raised a winged eyebrow in disbelief.

"I wouldn't have thought those memories were so unpleasant," he said innocently. "Unless you're talking about some other occasion than last Friday night."

"Damn it, there hasn't..." She trailed off, recognizing the look of satisfaction on his face. She'd fallen right into his trap. Quickly she finished her sentence. "There hasn't been any other *unpleasant* experience in that bed."

The gibe left him unmoved. "I wish you'd told me," he said plaintively. "I had the strange idea you enjoyed it as much as I did. I must have missed something."

"What do you want, Bran?" she demanded wearily, struggling to a sitting position, the comforter held loosely in front of her.

"I told you, we have some unfinished business,

Cassie. I thought we could spend the day together and sort some of it out.''

"I don't want to spend the day with you.''

"I'm sure you don't. And the sooner you indulge me, the sooner it will be over. That's what you want, isn't it? To have me leave you alone?''

"Yes,'' she replied with unflattering alacrity, still hesitating. "What exactly did you have in mind?''

His cynical smile deepened. "Nothing too terribly threatening. I've always wanted to explore the Oregon coast—check out the dunes and the sea stacks. We could spend the day by the ocean.''

She watched him out of wary eyes. "And what will your fiancée say to that?'' she countered.

"Lucy's gone back to Virginia. And believe it or not, she's not my fiancée.''

Cassie looked askance at his reasonable tone. "Oh, she isn't? I wonder what gave everyone that impression? Perhaps it was her proprietary manner. Not to mention that gaudy piece of jewelry she wears on her left hand.''

"I hate to shatter your innocence, Cassie, but there is more than one reason to give a woman an expensive piece of jewelry. It doesn't have to be a promise of eternal devotion—it can be an expression of gratitude for services rendered.'' His eyes narrowed in the bright morning sunlight. "What's so funny?''

Cassie hadn't been able to restrain a look of amusement. "That's exactly what I told her,'' she said giggling.

Bran was instantly alert, and Cassie could have cursed her flippancy. "When did you speak with her?" he demanded. "As far as I knew, the two of you kept your distance."

She hesitated. "I don't think it's any of your business."

"And I'm sure it's very much my business. I can't imagine anything else the two of you have in common, other than me. When did you see her?"

If she didn't give him some excuse, he'd nag at her until he found out, she realized wearily. "We had lunch together yesterday," she explained, albeit with obvious reluctance. "She wanted to warn me away from you. I wanted to assure her I had absolutely no interest in you whatsoever."

Disbelief was patent in his eyes, but a slow grin lit his mouth. "You wouldn't, by any chance, have had anything to do with a plate of pasta being dumped in her lap?"

Cassie did her best to keep a straight face, but the remembered delight of it was too strong for her. Her grin answered his. "It's a possibility," she admitted.

"God, I wish I'd been there to see it. She was still livid when she left." A low laugh escaped him. "But that doesn't mean I think you're telling me the whole truth. Who set up the meeting? I assume Lucy did." Cassie refused to acknowledge the question, and he continued on. "She must have had some other reason," he said meditatively. "It won't take me long to find out." He smiled sweetly at her, and Cassie felt a chill of premonition trickle down her spine.

But at least Lucy hadn't told him about Merrie. If Cassie could calm his suspicions, soothe his ruffled feelings, if such they were, then he would leave in the next two days none the wiser. "Your fiancée is a jealous woman," she said, stretching casually.

"She isn't my fiancée," he repeated patiently. "Are we going to spend the day together?"

Cassie eyed him, a light smile playing about her mouth. "I hadn't anything else planned," she allowed. "And I haven't been to the dunes in a while." That was a direct lie—she and Merrie had sat and watched the wind-swept sand for hours yesterday. And then she realized she had lost his attention for the moment.

He was staring at her breasts. Her casual yawn had dislodged the comforter, and the thin cotton T-shirt stretched over her round softness enticingly. As she felt her skin grow warm under his intent gaze, her nipples hardened in response to the heat in his eyes, and she pulled the T-shirt closer.

Of course, it only intensified the effect. "Virginia is for Lovers." He read the inscription softly. "I could have told you that, Cassie." One hand reached out to gently caress one soft breast.

She jerked away, burned by the tender touch. "We can spend the day together, and we can talk," she said hastily. "But that's all."

Slowly he withdrew his hand, his face, as always, unreadable. "All right."

"In the meantime, you can make yourself useful by making us some coffee. You woke me up," she accused him. "You have a nasty habit of doing that. I'll get dressed while you brew the coffee, and we can be on our way."

"Don't you eat breakfast? I would think a former nutrition researcher would know better than that."

Her eyes met his stonily. "My time as a nutrition researcher is not remembered with any particular affection," she said coldly. "As you could no doubt imagine, if you weren't such an insensitive pig. My coffee?"

He hesitated, then pulled himself out of the low-slung chair. "You still hate instant coffee?"

That memory almost undid her. "The beans are in the refrigerator, the electric grinder on the counter," she said huskily, waiting pointedly for him to leave the room. It wasn't until he was safely in the kitchen that she made the mad dash to her bedroom, clad only in the scanty T-shirt. His low whistle of appreciation from the kitchen door followed her fleeing figure.

"You know, I haven't yet apologized to you for doubting your integrity," he said. They were walking slowly along the beach just south of Bern, the shifting sands beneath their feet warm in the bright sunlight. It was too early in the season for the high winds to whip the tiny stinging grains into the blinding storms, as they did later in the summer, and a large patch of deep purple vetch was struggling valiantly to survive amid the shifting inhospitable dunes.

"I realized I was wrong soon after you left Virginia. By the time I got over being so mad at you for running off, I thought back to all that so-called evidence that had been trotted out for my inspection by Alleyn and Thompson. And it was all a bit too pat. It might comfort you to know that Thompson was just as duped as

I was. We both thought Alleyn's reputation was above reproach."

"And it was a lot easier to think the worst of me," she filled in bitterly. "After all, what did you have to lose? A first-year researcher is fairly expendable— possible Nobel prizewinners are a bit rarer."

"I don't blame you for being angry." He sounded positively subdued, and Cassie cast a surreptitious glance up at his shuttered expression. "I just wanted to apologize."

"I've forgotten it," she lied, shoving her hands in the pockets of her navy blue Windbreaker. She had deliberately stopped herself from dressing to please him. Her jeans were old and faded, her sneakers well-worn, and the high-necked rust-colored sweater had seen better days. What she had failed to recognize was that the slim-fitting jeans hugged her curves entic- ingly, so that Bran had a difficult time concentrating on the ever-shifting variety of the dunes, and the rust- colored sweater was the same one she'd worn two years ago, when she had first arrived at the Landover airport. It hugged her riper curves beneath the open Windbreaker, and it was all Bran could do to keep from grabbing her. He followed her example, stuffing his long strong hands into the pockets of his jeans.

"There's something more I want to say about that whole mess," he said after a long moment. "I did what I could to make it up to you."

This penetrated her abstraction. "What do you mean?"

"Did you suppose Alleyn was stupid enough to keep making the same mistakes without a little help?"

he demanded cynically. "He knew he'd barely escaped disgrace—he was a very careful man for the next six months or so. Unfortunately for him, he didn't realize he was up against me." While leaning down Bran picked up a fragment of driftwood and stared at it as if it held the answers of the universe.

"Through my blind stupidity I'd had all the incriminating evidence destroyed," he continued. "Evidence that, if checked and double-checked by experts skilled at uncovering research fraud, could have proved your innocence. So my only option was to set up a situation where he'd cheat again, and this time catch him at it. A sting operation, if you will." The wind was ruffling his hair around his high tanned forehead, and it was all Cassie could do to stop herself from reaching up and smoothing the tangled locks back.

"And it worked?" she queried, trying to keep her mind on his narrative.

"Child's play," Bran verified. "Dr. Stanley Alleyn was pretty well convinced he was infallible. The Foundation dangled a substantial grant in front of his nose, one that depended on well-researched preliminary data. Alleyn, in his eagerness for that grant and his conviction that no one could possibly doubt a scientist of his stature, supplied the data—a much more blatant forgery than the first, as a matter of fact. And he had a scapegoat already selected. A friend of yours named Eliza Barnett."

"Eliza! How dare he! That unprincipled, sneaking—"

Bran broke into her tirade. "Alleyn didn't realize that Eliza had offered me her assistance at the begin-

ning of my little project. The moment he realized that
she was helping me, he collapsed. I think the blow to
his ego was far worse than his destroyed reputation,"
he added meditatively. He tossed the piece of driftwood out toward the ocean, his eyes narrowed in the
sunlight.

"But I've spoken with Eliza several times in the
past year," Cassie said, eyeing him warily. "She never
mentioned a thing."

"I asked her not to—not that she'd tell me a thing
about you." There was a slightly aggrieved note in his
voice. "A very stubborn woman, Miss Eliza Barnett."

"*Ms.* Eliza Barnett," she supplied automatically.
"And indeed she is," she added, a wave of relief
spreading through her at his answer to her unspoken
question. "Why did you bother to ask her?"

He seemed to withdraw into himself. "Curiosity,"
he said shortly, shrugging.

If his terse answer hurt, Cassie managed to hide it
admirably. "Well, anyway, thank you for doing what
you did. Belated trust is better than no trust at all."
Her words were deliberately cruel, and as his wintry
eyes met hers, he responded in kind.

"The reputation of the Foundation was at stake,
too," Bran said in an unmoved voice.

"I'm sure that was your major concern," she
agreed sweetly. "Do you want to head down to Brandon?" The change in subject was scarcely subtle, but
she was past caring. "The sea stacks are really magnificent down there—these gorgeous pinnacles looming in the ocean. They're one of the things I love most
about the Oregon coast."

He accepted the change of subject equably enough. "You do like it here?" he queried. "You're happy?"

For the life of her, Cassie couldn't figure out why it would matter to him, but she nodded. "Yes, I've been very happy." Whether she would be again was a different matter. Somehow she doubted that the violent coast of Oregon would ever provide the solace she had once found in abundance. She slanted a mocking grin up at him. "Why? Did you hope I was pining away for you?"

"That seemed unlikely, since you were the one who chose to leave," he said in a somber tone. "I still don't accept your reasons. Certain things are more important than silly pride."

"To you, perhaps. There's also a small matter of self-respect, dignity, trust—"

"Why did you change your mind?" he interrupted.

"Change my mind?" she echoed, puzzled. "What makes you think I changed my mind?"

"Why else did you call me? I asked Lucy, and she said she did vaguely remember a mysterious female calling me sometime in the middle of the night last winter."

"There's that lovely question of trust again," she said ironically. "It's nice to know my word is sacred to you."

"You still haven't answered me. Why did you call me, unless you happened to be missing me, having second thoughts about running off?" He was inexorable.

"Let's go to Brandon," she said, starting away from him. She should have known she wouldn't get very far. A moment later he had pulled her up against his taut length, his eyes blazing down into hers, his mouth hovering enticingly above her lips. "Why, Cassie?" he whispered.

She felt trapped, mesmerized by the flaming desire she saw written on his face. All it would take was a word, even a nod, and that mouth would come down on hers, sealing his possession of her very soul. One word, and she was lost, forever, and gladly so. But it wasn't only her life—it was Merrie's too, and Bran could be an implacable enemy.

She wet her suddenly dry lips, averting her eyes. "I was trying to get in touch with Meredith," she said evenly, her heart pounding, and with aching regret she felt his hold loosen, until she was once more standing on her own.

"Then why didn't you ask for her?" His voice was flat, discouraged. He believed her, she thought with amazement. How could he be so gullible? Couldn't he feel the way her heart raced whenever he held her, see the way her skin flushed and hands trembled when he came close? And why didn't she feel more of a sense of triumph?

"Because hearing Lucy's voice flustered me. I was expecting to have to talk to you, which I really didn't want to do, and then when Lucy answered, I just said the first thing that popped into my mind."

She could feel him staring down at her, feel the tension and frustration emanating from his wiry body. More than anything she longed to go back into those arms, thread her arms around his lean waist and lay her head against the strong, commanding warmth of his chest. Bravely she met his quizzical gaze, keeping her own expression calm and reasonable.

"I'll take you home," he said abruptly.

She was startled. "I thought you wanted to see the Oregon coast? The sea stacks up by Bern are nothing compared to the ones farther south."

"I'm no longer in the mood for sight-seeing." Bran's voice was weary. "I have a great deal to do if I'm going to leave Monday. I shouldn't have taken today off from work."

"You're leaving Monday?" Cassie felt oddly shaken. She knew he would go soon—she wanted him to leave—but the thought of his imminent departure left her feeling bereft. She would have Merrie back, she reminded herself. That would be more than enough, wouldn't it?

The ride back to Bern was accomplished in absolute silence. It was already late afternoon and as they drove up the coastal route Cassie watched the giant red ball of the sun sink slowly toward the sea, and she wondered if there was anything she could say to lighten the tension between the two of them, so that they could part as friends. Sometime she would have to tell him—her conscience was too strong to allow her to keep silent forever. And it would be so much easier if there could be at least a semblance of amity between the two of them. But the stony set of his mouth, the wintry cast to his usually blazing eyes, told their story. There was nothing she could say that could turn them into casual friends—too much had gone on between them already.

"You don't have to see me to my door," she said

hastily as she reached for the handle of his rented Mercedes. He ignored her, however, following her up the winding stone steps to her front door. He stood there, towering over her and making her feel little, helpless, and insignificant while she fumbled for her key in the small canvas purse she carried. She finally found it, nestled under one of Merrie's pacifiers. After grabbing the key, she quickly closed the purse away from any possible prying eyes.

Bran, however, noticed nothing, all his concentration on other things. Before Cassie realized what was happening she found herself pushed up against the door, Bran's strong body pinning her there as his mouth reached down and ravaged hers.

The sudden savagery of his kiss caught her off guard. By their own volition her arms went up around his neck, drawing him closer to her trembling body, and she answered his kiss fully, lost in the heaven-hell of his mouth on hers, his lean hips pressing against her, his arms strong and firm and demanding. And then, as suddenly as it began, it was over. He pulled away, and she let him go, reluctantly, her arms falling to her sides, her mouth bruised and swollen, her eyes wide.

"Good-bye, Cassie." And without another word he turned on his heels and bounded down the stone steps two at a time. A moment later the afternoon fog swallowed up the Mercedes, leaving her alone in the quiet stillness.

Chapter Eighteen

The rain began that night, a steady monotonous downpour that pounded on the cedar-shingled roof of Cassie's retreat, beat against the windows, and washed over the balconies in sheets of gray water. Cassie did what she could to survive the desperate gloom engendered by the weather and her life.

Cassie rose late on Sunday, dressing up in velvet pants and a velour top, treating herself to a fire and brandied coffee and a good book. The velvet pants picked up lint from the carpet when she tried to lie down in front of the fireplace. The velour top itched her skin. The wood in the fireplace hissed and spat and smoked, doing little to warm the gloomy afternoon, the brandy reminded her of nights in Virginia, and the damn book turned out to be a romance. So after her valiant effort, Cassie gave in. Lying in front of the fire, staring out into the rain-swept afternoon, she tried to figure out how she could have handled things differently and where she had gone wrong.

Monday dawned cold and cheerless, with the heavy rain waiting in the wings to resume again. This would

be the last day without Merrie, Cassie told herself as
she dressed for courage in her most flattering and dignified clothing—a beige linen suit with a slit skirt that
showed a nice expanse of slender thigh. After tonight
she could go fetch her baby, and she would never
have to worry about Bran Rathburne again. She could
only hope that things could return to normal.

She went through the day in a tense fog equal to the
mist outside her office windows. Every time the
phone rang she expected it to be Bran. Every knock
on her door, every sound of approaching footsteps,
made her start in panic, only to subside in disappointment. She saw him once, just after lunch, from a distance, deep in conversation with Dr. Gibson and a
studiously polite David Tremayne. He looked up, and
from across the wide expanse of the Cooper lunch-
room his silver-blue gaze caught hers. They stared at
each other for what seemed an eternity. "I love you,"
Cassie told him silently, her eyes wide and desperate.
He turned his attention back to David, turning his tall
beautiful back as well.

The very last thing she wanted to do was say good-
bye to him. That afternoon she threw herself into her
work, checking and rechecking the results of the latest
experiments, this time dealing with the Bach Flower
Remedies and their possible healing powers. She had
neglected her work for too long, spent too much time
seeking heartsease and not enough time working with
it. She decided to work well past six o'clock, then
drive straight to June's ranch house. Bran would have
to take the five o'clock flight—it was the last one out,
and David had made it clear that morning that Bran

was determined not to spend another night in Oregon.

Five o'clock came and went, with Cassie glancing at the clock only every three minutes. Slowly but steadily the laboratories emptied, until she was all alone in her office, staring sightlessly at the reports as she listened to the rain that had begun just before five.

At six-thirty she rose, stretched, and slipped off her lab coat, running tired fingers through her thick curtain of chestnut hair. He was gone—she and Merrie were safe. It was a time for celebrating. Everything had its price, and she had just paid it. Regrets would get her nowhere—she would do it all over again.

There were still several cars out in the parking lot, although in the pouring rain Cassie couldn't make out which ones they were. She raced to her secondhand Fiat, yanked open the door, and dived inside. Merrie's car seat was safely locked in the trunk. She'd picked the lock on the nursery door this morning and put fresh sheets on the crib. Everything was in readiness.

After starting the car, always sluggish in the heavy rain, she turned on the headlights, put the gears in reverse, and began to back up. A moment later there was a sickening crunch, the sound of crushed metal and broken glass, and her car stalled out. In the rain-shrouded light of her headlights she could see the rented Mercedes pulled directly behind her, its left headlight smashed and darkened.

In sudden panic Cassie locked the doors, then turned the key to start the car once more. A useless whirring sound greeted her desperate attempts. She should have known. The Fiat, of a venerable age, had

its little quirks, one of which was a refusal to start
more than once in a rainstorm. On the stormy Oregon
coast she had had more than enough chances to dis-
cover this less than endearing trait.

"Come on, damn you," she muttered, turning the
key with all her strength, so that her fingers were
numb. She knew from the fading sound of the engine
that she was draining the battery, but she couldn't
help herself. The loud knocking on her window was
the final straw. Bran stood there, hatless, coatless, in
the pouring rain, and there was nothing she could do
but unlock the car door, pulling the key from the ignition and turning off the lights with numbed resignation.

Without a word he took her reluctant arm, leading
her toward his car. The Mercedes was sturdy enough
to withstand what damage an elderly Fiat could inflict.
She wished she could say the same for her car. The
back was caved in. There would be no opening of the
trunk to retrieve Merrie's car seat—at least, not without a can opener. In sudden rage she yanked her arm
out of Bran's light grip, halting by the side of his car,
oblivious to the rain that plastered her linen suit to
her body, drenched her hair, and filled her shoes.

"I'm not going anywhere with you," she shouted
above the noise of the storm. "You were supposed to
have been gone by now."

"I would have been, but the airport was closed due
to heavy winds," he shouted back. "I decided to try
with you one more time. You have to let me drive you
home. You have no other way to get there." Once
more he caught her arm, and this time there was no

way she could break free of his iron grip as he bundled her into the car.

A moment later he was in the driver's seat beside her. The rain had plastered his curly black hair to his skull, soaked the thin cotton shirt he wore, and suddenly Cassie felt the last bit of fight drain from her. She watched him with a curious sense of fatality. She had fought, but fate seemed to be decreeing that she would lose.

"You'll get the seat drenched," she said quietly. "So will I."

"I think the rental company will be more concerned about the front fender," he said wryly, his eyes warm in the dimly lit interior of the car. "I hadn't realized you'd be backing out quite so fast."

"Did you mean to hit me?" She was no more than idly curious at this point. She had accepted whatever life chose to hand her.

"Yes. Not quite so hard, of course. But I meant to stop you any way I could."

She nodded absently, leaning back against the wet leather seat and staring out into the rain-swept landscape. "Are you going to drive me home?" she asked evenly.

"If you'll let me." The look he slanted across at her was curious, subdued, and strangely hopeful.

"Oh, I'll let you," she said passively.

He started the car, put it into gear, and with a small unpleasant sound of scrunching metal, pulled away from Cassie's dented car. They were speeding down the highway before he spoke again. "Why the sudden capitulation?"

She kept her eyes straight ahead. "I've given up fighting," she said wearily. "It doesn't seem to do any good."

"I could have told you that before, if you'd bothered to listen." There was no smugness in that husky drawling voice, only a strange kind of relief. Absently Cassie wondered what he was relieved about. Relief at finally getting his own way, at her surrender? And for what? Pride? Revenge? Or something more positive? He had once, long ago, told her he was falling in love with her. Had those small traces of emotion vanished with the passage of time? And what good would it do her if they hadn't?

She watched numbly as he pulled around her driveway and into the garage beneath the house. When he finally stopped the car, he turned to her, his eyes glittering in the half-light.

"The first thing you need to do," he said gently enough, "is to get out of those wet clothes and into a hot bath. You go on ahead, and I'll find some brandy to warm you."

"I don't need—" she began incoherently, but he leaned over and kissed her, briefly, gently, stopping her protests.

"You'll catch pneumonia," he said softly. "You've been working much too hard, not eating enough, and you've been under considerable stress. And if you wonder how I know this, it's because I've been going through the same thing. Now, humor me for a change, and do as I say. Please." The last was tacked on almost as an afterthought, and Cassie nodded obediently, not even able to fight this small battle. She would do whatever he told her to do, as she had somehow lost the capacity to think for herself, somewhere along the way.

Ten minutes later she was up to her neck in soap bubbles in the sybaritically deep tub the retired couple had uncharacteristically included in their house plans. Her wet clothes were in a sodden heap on the bathroom carpeting, her hair was tied in a haphazard knot on the top of her head, and she leaned back against the tub, closing her eyes in delight at the restful feel of the warm lavender-scented water against her skin. And then she opened them again as she felt Bran's liquid gaze on her.

He was lounging negligently against the side of the bathroom door, two brandy snifters in his hands, his sodden shirt still intact. With his usual pantherlike grace he moved into the steam-clouded bathroom, placing one snifter in her limp hand and resting the other on the vanity. A moment later he was pulling his wet shirt free from his pants, tossing it on top of her pile of clothing.

Cassie stared at his bronzed damp chest in sudden shyness. "What are you doing?" she whispered as his hands went to his belt buckle, and the belt followed the shirt onto the pile.

"I was thinking of joining you," he murmured, a slow smile lighting his face. "But I don't think there'd be room in that tub for me, too." He pulled a thick towel from the rack and began to dry his hair-matted stomach, then rubbed it briskly through his wet curls. "I'll just have to wait until you come out."

"Wait for what?"

"For you," he said gently, leaning against the vanity and picking up his brandy once more. "Sip your drink."

Dutifully she obeyed him, the warm brandy blazing a trail down her throat, warming the last, small cold part of her. Looking up at him out of warm, luminous, honey-brown eyes, she saw a spasm of pain cross his face. And then he was on his knees beside the tub, his hands gently cupping her face.

"I love you, you know," he said softly, desperately, and her heart blazed in hopeless triumph. "I came here to get you out of my system, and you only got more deeply embedded. I can't go away and leave you—I need you too much to ever be without you again. I want to marry you, Cassie, if you'll have me. I love you." And his mouth caught hers, his kiss deep, reverent, and pleading.

After reaching up, she covered his hands with hers, opening her mouth beneath his gentle insistence, tasting the sweet tenderness of his mouth as he tasted hers. For long breathless moments they kissed, until Bran moved his lips away to graze her cheekbones, her nose, her chin, and her fluttering eyelids. And each kiss was a benediction, a vow, a promise of trust—a trust she had already betrayed.

The shrill ringing of the telephone pulled them apart, and Bran laughed ruefully. "I'll get it." Before she could gather her dazed senses he was gone, and it took her precious moments to realize it could be someone incriminating—June, wondering where she was, for instance. She jumped out of the tub and grabbed a bath sheet and ran into the living room, her bare wet feet leaving footprints on the thick carpet.

"Here she is, Dr. Gibson," he spoke into the telephone, then held the receiver out to her. "It's your boss," he said lightly. "Some after-hours crisis."

With shaking hands she took the phone from him, one hand trying to keep the towel from slipping off her nude body. Bran was no help at all as she tried to take in the details of Dr. Gibson's agitated voice. Bran's mouth was trailing hot moist kisses along her neck, down her shoulder blade, his tongue snaking out at intervals to further tantalize her bath-warmed skin.

"One moment, sir. I need a pencil." With a mock glare she waved Bran away, mouthing the word *pencil* at him. "What was that, sir? One moment, Mr. Rathburne is finding me something to write with. Just a moment." She turned to see what was keeping him, and her heart stopped beating.

Bran had gone to the most logical place to find a writing implement. Her purse had been lying on a nearby chair, and he'd picked it up, rummaging through it for a pencil. He'd come up with the pacifier, and he was standing there, staring at it in stunned silence.

And then his eyes met her agonized ones for a long considering moment. Before she could stop him he turned, heading directly for what had been locked to him the last time he was there.

"I'm sorry, Dr. Gibson, I've had an emergency of my own," she mumbled into the phone. "Call Dr. Tremayne." And before he could do more than protest she'd slammed the phone down, racing after Bran's tall figure.

He was standing in the middle of Merrie's room, staring about him with unseeing eyes. The story it told was clear enough, from the embroidered birth announcement to the blown-up picture June had taken of Cassie and Merrie on Merrie's first birthday. He turned to stare at her then, and the pain in his blue eyes was so intense, it was like a physical blow. And all Cassie could do was to stare back helplessly, lost for any word of comfort or explanation.

Chapter Nineteen

His voice when he spoke was full of anguish, and the sound of it was like a whiplash on her soul. "How old is she?"

She wet her suddenly dry lips, "Fifteen months." It came out as little more than a whisper.

"I'm not going to bother with any crap about mathematics," he said, his voice low and furious. "Were you pregnant when you were in Virginia?"

The time for prevarication was past. "I wasn't when I got there," she said honestly. "Apparently, I was by the time I left."

Bran shut his eyes for a moment, as if the sight of Cassie was more than he could bear. And then he crossed the room in a few short strides, his fingers digging into the soft, tender flesh of her upper arms as he shook her so hard, she thought her neck might snap.

"Damn you, damn you, damn you!" he swore, his voice raw. And then he released her, pushing her from him in disgust. "You really must have hated me, far more than I could even begin to guess. Was it a good enough revenge for you, Cassie, to bear my child and keep her from me? To have my flesh and blood and hoard her, deny her a father, deny her a family, all for your own stupid pride and hatred?''

"I didn't..." she began faintly, her voice fading out, then getting stronger with determination. "I tried to tell you. It was just a week after her birth that I tried to call you and Lucy answered."

"Your belated conscience is admirable, but it sure as hell didn't hold up to much stress. And what were you doing all the time you were pregnant that you couldn't let me know? Trying to find someone to abort you at a late stage?''

"Damn you, no!" she cried. "I knew I should tell you. I wanted to tell you. But I was afraid you'd try and take her away from me."

"You were right." His voice was filled with white-hot rage, his eyes blazing with hatred and contempt as he spoke the words that were her death knell. "And if you think you have a chance in hell against the Rathburne name and fortune, you can think again. I'll have my daughter from you so fast, your head will spin."

"No, Bran," she begged piteously, all pride abandoning her. "Please, try to understand. I know you're angry, I know you hate me for not telling you, but I had my reasons."

"I don't give a damn what they are," he shot back. "I don't think I've ever come closer to wanting to kill someone in my entire life. Where is my daughter?"

Cassie met his rage unflinchingly. "I'm not going to tell you."

He took one menacing step toward her. "I suggest you don't goad me, Cassie. I'm so angry, I could very easily hurt you quite badly, and I wouldn't want to do that. It might make it a little more difficult to get custody of—What's her damn name?"

"Meredith."

"Damn you," he said again, more quietly now. "Where is she? Are you going to tell me, or am I going to have to beat it out of you?"

There was little choice. "She's staying with my sister."

"Where?" he barked.

"I'm not going to tell you," she repeated, her voice gaining strength.

He stared at her for a long furious moment. "It doesn't matter. It'll take me an hour, two at the most, to have her name and address."

"Bran, don't..." She put out a restraining hand, but he moved out of her way as if she had the plague.

"Don't touch me," he ordered fiercely. "Don't even come near me. I don't want to hurt you, but I swear if you come near me, I might." He stared at her for a long moment, and then, almost in slow motion, he reached out and slammed his fist against the door.

Cassie heard the wood splinter beneath the impact, and she flinched. And then he was gone, the door slamming behind him as he disappeared into the stormy night.

Her knees buckled underneath her in sudden reaction, and she found herself on the floor, the towel still clasped uselessly around her rapidly chilling body. The moment she had dreaded for so long had finally

come, and it was worse, far worse than she had anticipated. For once she fully deserved the hatred and contempt he showered upon her. As she knelt there, her
head bowed in guilt and anguish, the sight of one of
Merrie's tiny red sneakers intruded on her misery.
She stared at it, mesmerized, and then with sudden
resolution her head snapped up.

She wasn't going to give up Merrie without a fight.
As much as she deserved his hatred, she wasn't going
to acquiesce, hand over her child with a mumbled
apology. No, he'd have to fight for her. And she could
be just as formidable as any damn Rathburne, she
thought.

Her determination suffered a tiny check when
June's number proved busy every time she tried it.
Willing herself to stay calm, Cassie went into her bedroom and threw on an old pair of corduroys and a
flannel shirt. She would simply drive over there and
fetch Merrie. It would take Bran at least until tomorrow morning to locate June, if he did at all. In the
meantime she and Merrie could be far away—

"Oh, no!" The words escaped her as she suddenly
remembered just where her car was—stalled out in
the Cooper Laboratories' parking lot, and no earthly
good to her at all.

It took longer for the panic to subside this time. It
wasn't until David's pleasant voice answered the
fourth ring that she finally gained control.

"David, I need your help," she said without preamble.

"Sandra, what's wrong?" He was instantly concerned.

"I—I—" To her shame the tears threatened to choke her. Determinedly she swallowed them. "David, I'm in trouble. I need you to come pick me up at home and take me to my car. I left it parked at work." She took a deep shaky breath. "I'll explain what I can when you get here."

"Does this have something to do with Merrie?" he questioned shrewdly.

"You might say so," she admitted. "How did you know?"

"Elementary. She's the only thing you could get so upset over. Is she all right?"

"For now. But I need to get my car so I can go pick her up at June's. Please, David, hurry! I—I'm frightened."

"I'll be right there."

But even driving with uncharacteristic haste, David couldn't possibly get there for at least fifteen minutes. Add the rain and the fog, and Cassie couldn't really expect him for close to a half hour. And then another fifteen minutes to Cooper, twenty minutes to June's... If Bran's sources were even half as efficient as he had claimed, she was cutting it close, she knew. Once more she dialed June's number, only to have the same frustrating busy signal echo in her ears.

After slamming down the phone, she quickly dialed the operator. "I need an emergency interrupt," she spoke rapidly. "I'm trying to get through to my sister. Our mother is desperately ill, and her line has been busy for the last hour." She lied without compunction, giving June's number twice as her tongue stumbled over the numbers.

"I'm sorry, that number is out of order," the dis-embodied voice came back to her, stripping her of her last hope. After mumbling a dazed thanks, Cassie dropped the phone back in its cradle.

"Please, God," she murmured out loud. "Don't let him find her."

She was standing out in the heavy drizzle when finally, an anguished forty-five minutes later, David's stately Bonneville drove in her driveway. Before he could even come to a stop she had raced down the stone steps, her sneakered feet sliding dangerously on the wet, slick stone. She yanked the car door open and scrambled inside as David was in the act of turning off the ignition.

"David, please!" she begged, her eyes huge and frightened in her pale face.

Obediently he put the car in gear again, pulling out of her driveway onto the narrow road with maddening deliberation. "I'm sorry I'm so late, Sandra," he said, a note of worry in his face. "But Dr. Gibson phoned me just as I was leaving. There's a minor crisis in the herbal project, and he—"

"I know all about it. He was trying to explain it to me when—when something happened," she interrupted him, perched on the edge of her seat, her eyes peering through the rain-swept darkness.

"So he told me," Divid said dryly. "I assured him I'd take care of it—you had enough on your mind. He also mentioned an odd phone call from Bran Rathburne."

The prickling on the edges of her nerves should have warned her, combined with the nauseous feeling in the pit of her stomach. "When did Bran call him?"

"Right before he called me. He couldn't figure it out—he thought Rathburne was at your place. But he obviously couldn't have been. And I thought he'd taken the five o'clock flight back east." David shook his head confusedly, and it was all Cassie could do to stop from reaching out and pressing her sneakered foot down on his accelerator pedal.

"What did he want?" There was resignation and a deep sadness in her voice. The game was almost over, and she, undoubtedly, had lost. Everything.

"For some odd reason he wanted June's name and address."

"And did he give it to him?"

"Of course he did. The Rathburne Foundation is thinking of giving Cooper a great deal of money—Gibson could hardly have refused a reasonable request like that. But I fail to see—Sandra, are you crying?" His voice softened with sudden concern.

Slowly, wearily, she leaned back against the plush seat, the hot tears streaming unheeded down her face. "It doesn't matter," she said weakly. "It's too late to do anything about it."

"Sandra, what's going on?" There was no demand in David's voice, just gentle solicitude. It was that solicitude she gathered herself to respond to.

"Bran Rathburne is Merrie's father," she said slowly, simply. "He didn't know of her existence until about an hour ago."

A deep indrawn breath signified his shock. "And that's why Merrie has been staying with June?"

Miserably, she nodded. "I was trying to keep her

out of his way. I thought we had it made. If only he'd caught that plane today!''

"You should have told him, Sandra." David's voice was deep with reproach. "A man has a right to know he has a child. He has feelings and needs, too, you know. I think if I were in his place, I'd have a hard time forgiving you, too."

"Damn it, his contribution lasted maybe a half hour!" she shot back. "I carried her for nine months, I delivered her after twenty-three hours of labor, alone!"

"It was your decision to be alone," he reminded her implacably. "And none of that alters the facts. She is his child as much as yours, and you've kept her from him."

The guilt that was never far from her washed over her once more. "If you don't mind, I'd rather not talk about it," she said wearily. "I'm paying for my mistakes, I don't need you to tell me how immoral I've been." She took a deep tired breath. "I already know it."

"What happened to your car?" They had finally pulled up outside Cooper Laboratories, and in the light of the high beams Cassie could make out the sickeningly crunched fender and trunk of her car. There would be no getting the car seat from back there—she'd somehow have to manage getting Merrie home without any kind of restraint. If she was still at June's, that is, she realized.

"I had a slight accident," she mumbled, sliding out of the front seat into the pouring rain. "And then it stalled out—you know the problems I've had with this old car. I'm sure it will start now. All it usually needs is a rest.''

And bless its tired old engine, it did, after a fitful cough and sputter. David was standing by her open window, the rain plastering down his fair hair and covering his glasses with thick droplets. ''Are you going to be all right?'' he asked, concern deep in his voice.

''I suppose so. I'll call you in the morning. I—I'm not sure if I'll be in to work.''

He nodded, and then suddenly leaned down and kissed her, lightly, chastely, on her rain-damp cheek. ''Drive carefully, Sandra.''

Easy enough to say, she thought in anguish as she sped through the rain-swept streets. It wasn't his child she was rushing to, not his life that was crumbling before her eyes.

She was on the quiet residential street that held June's rambling ranch house, a few short blocks away, when a car loomed out of the darkness, one headlight out. As it sped past her, she saw Bran's grim face reflected in the streetlights. He was staring straight ahead, his expression carved of granite, and then he was gone into the night.

She hit June's garbage cans as she screeched to a stop outside her brightly lit house. Garbage was strewn everywhere on the manicured rain-drenched lawn, but she paid no attention. The door opened to her desperate pounding, and she fell into the warm bright living room.

''Cassie, my heavens...'' June's worried voice came to her from a distance. But all she could see was her daughter's cherubic face beaming up at her from her seat on the carpet, and Merrie held out chubby arms to her mother with an expression of absolute glee.

She swept down on her, grabbing her tiny body in her arms and holding her so tightly, Merrie squeaked in protest before chuckling at the strange new game her mother was playing. "Thank heavens he didn't find you," she murmured brokenly against her daughter's sweet-smelling black silky hair. "Thank heavens."

Slowly June closed the door, moving to stand beside her younger sister, a troubled expression on her pretty face. The two of them looked a great deal alike. June's hair was artificially blonder, her eyes a lighter brown, almost hazel, and her shorter body blessed with fifteen pounds she neither wanted nor needed. Now as she looked at her sister's bent head her light brown eyes were dark with concern.

"He did find her, Cassie," she said gently.

Cassie raised stricken eyes to her sister's face. "No," she whispered in hopeless protest. "What did he say? What did he do?"

June shook her blond curls. "He didn't say a word. I knew who he was, of course. You're right—you can't mistake those eyes. When I opened the door, he saw Merrie sitting there, and he pushed right past me. You know how shy Merrie can be sometimes?" At Cassie's nod she continued. "Well, she took to him right away, almost as if she knew who he was. He went over to her and picked her up, very gently, and then sat on the couch with her."

"And then?" Cassie's voice was hoarse with pain.

"Nothing. He just sat there, holding her, for about a half hour. And, oh, Cassie, he was crying! It just about broke my heart, seeing such a strong, powerful-looking man just sit there and hold his daughter and cry."

If Cassie thought she couldn't hurt anymore, she was wrong. June's words seared through her, and she stared down at the child she loved so much, wondering how she would ever find the strength to give her up. And then she noticed the smear of red on Merrie's terry sleeper.

"Is this blood?" she demanded harshly, her voice thick with her own tears.

June nodded. "He'd hurt his hand somehow. He said he ran into a door. I offered to bandage it for him, but he just looked right through me. Oh, Cassie, what in the world are you going to do? I feel so sorry for the poor man. But I don't want us to lose Merrie."

"We're not going to lose Merrie," Cassie said, suddenly feeling stronger, more determined.

"Are you going to go away? Someplace where he'll never find you? He might forget after a while—give up. But I don't really think so, Cassie. You didn't see his face."

"Yes, I did," she said quietly. "And he won't give up. But I'm not going to run. I'm not going to let him take her away from me, but he's owed something. She's his daughter; he has rights."

"I tried to tell you that before—" June began.

"And I didn't listen," Cassie supplied wearily. "I know all the mistakes I've made. I'm just going to have to do my best to remedy what I can of the situation. I'll take Merrie home and wait until I hear from his lawyers. It shouldn't take long. It only took him a half hour to find Merrie, once he knew of her existence. I'd expect a summons on my desk in less than twenty-four hours."

"You'd better find a lawyer yourself, Cass. You can't give her up without a fight."

"I told you, I'm not about to. But I can't refuse to let him see her, either. David will know of a good lawyer, I'm sure. Somehow we'll work this thing out." Her words sounded far more hopeful than she felt. "In the meantime, do you suppose you could get Merrie's clothes together for me?" She looked down at her daughter's tiny scowl. "I'm taking her home."

Chapter Twenty

The next three weeks were a hell Cassie doubted she could ever survive' again. She called David the next morning, only to find that Bran had left the state, undoubtedly driving all night with a smashed car and a damaged hand. Cassie took three days off to try to pull herself and her life back together again. It was a wasted effort. A week after she returned to work, the word came in from the Rathburne Foundation. The grant had been approved, and there was no word from Bran or his lawyers for Cassie.

As the first week slipped into the second Cassie found some of her panic lessening. David found her a lawyer—a good one named Hank Palmer, who specialized in custody cases. He wasn't able to make promises, but he assured her it was highly unlikely she would lose custody of her daughter, although sharing her was almost a certainty, unless she could prove he'd make an unfit father.

"No," she said quietly. "He'd make a very good father." The image of Bran holding his daughter, tears filling his silver-blue eyes, had haunted her days, tortured her nights.

"And of course he'll want to contribute to her support," Hank Palmer added.

Cassie had immediately stiffened. "I don't want a penny of his money."

"It wouldn't be for you, Ms. Thayer. It would be for your daughter."

"I don't care. I wouldn't touch it if we were starving," she declared, the thought of Bran's largess making her feel somehow soiled. "If there's no way I can avoid it, I'll put it in trust for Merrie when she's ready for college. But we don't need his help."

"I'm afraid, Ms. Thayer, that whether you need his help or not, you're probably going to get it."

And so she waited for the lawyer's call that never came. And the second week slipped into the third, and there was still no word.

During the third week the rain started. Every morning Cassie would look in vain for a trace of sun in the cloudy June sky, and every day she would accept the gray skies with leaden submission. The continued gloom of the weather made tempers short at Cooper Laboratories, and even June was less than her placid self when Cassie would go to fetch Merrie at the end of the workday.

Finally, almost a month after Bran had stormed out of her life, a Sunday morning dawned clear and bright, the hazy sunshine beginning the long task of drying out the sodden landscape. Cassie and Merrie spent the day on the rock-strewn beach, gathering and discarding driftwood as it took their fancies, feeding

the gulls, collecting shells. Merrie was still a bit unsteady on her feet, preferring to have her mother
carry her over the uneven terrain, so that by the time
they got back to the wood-and-stone house, Cassie's
back and arms ached, her feet were tired, and for the
first time in many weeks she began to feel at peace.

A cool shower washed some of the sand and salt
stickiness from her skin. She was dressed in a flowing
cotton sundress with a blissful nothing underneath it,
and was in the kitchen starting dinner for herself and
Merrie, when she heard the car.

She peered out the window, but no one was in sight.
The entire landscape was bathed in a pinkish-rose hue
from the vibrant sunset, warming the drowned grass
and lending a soft glow to the winding driveway. It
was a magic time of day, and Cassie felt the rough grip
of tension easing from around her heart.

"Must have been my imagination, Merrie," she
informed her daughter, who, oblivious to her mother's abstraction, was playing by her bare feet. "I
guess I should learn to concentrate, shouldn't I, darling?"

Merrie grinned up in agreement, just as the front
doorbell rang. The sound sent a shock of panic
through Cassie, one that she stilled forcibly. She had
to stop jumping like a frightened rabbit every time the
phone rang, every time someone came to her door,
she admonished herself. If she hadn't heard from
Bran in four weeks, it was unlikely that he was going
to bother her now. He'd probably been so full of disgust that he couldn't even bear to think about their
untenable situation, she decided.

The bell pealed once more, and, scooping her daughter up from the floor, Cassie strode to the door, Merrie balanced on one hip. She could only be grateful she had something to hold on to when the door opened to reveal Merrie's father.

He looked as if he'd been through as deep a hell as she had. There were new lines etched around his grim unsmiling mouth, radiating about the chilly silver-blue eyes, grooved in the sides of his lean tanned cheeks. There were more shadows under his eyes, and his black hair seemed even more liberally sprinkled with gray. She stared at him, unaware of the moving picture she made, her long slim legs bare beneath the cotton sundress, her child in her arms. His expression seemed to harden.

Cassie had absolutely no idea what to say to him. She wanted to burst into tears, to beg his forgiveness, to plead for mercy. She just stood there and stared at him, silently, until Merrie mercifully broke the silence.

With a shout of joy she launched herself forward, her chubby arms reaching out for him, her gap-toothed smile wide in her round face. His strong slender hands reached out and caught her deftly, as if catching babies were a common occurrence, and he held her small body against him with a gentleness that was all the more touching because of the leashed strength in his leanly muscled frame. Cassie felt her throat close with sudden strong emotion.

Finally, he spoke. "I thought it was more than time we talked."

She cleared her throat, once, twice. "All right," she

agreed. "As soon as I've fed Merrie she'll go to sleep for the night, and then we can—"

"Not here," he interrupted. "I think we'd better have this discussion on neutral ground. I don't trust myself on your home turf."

She hesitated for a long moment. "All right," she said again. "I'll feed Merrie, and we can—"

"No. You can find someone to come in and stay with her while we go out and talk. I don't want her with us while we sort this out."

"She won't know what we're talking about, Bran," Cassie argued reasonably.

"No. I realize that I haven't any say in her life at this point, but you could indulge me this once," he said cynically. "Call a baby-sitter."

"But I'm not sure if I can find one on such short notice." A part of her was terrified at the thought of placing herself in his hands, alone. His hurt and rage had been very deep—had they lasted?

Apparently, they had. "If you care about the custody of your daughter, you'll find one soon enough." He started toward the living room, still carrying Merrie in his arms. "We'll leave as soon as she's fed and settled for the night."

Bran left her little choice. "All right," she agreed, subdued. "Do you want a drink while you're waiting?"

"No." The word was sharp, short, telling her quite clearly that he wanted nothing from her but the one thing she wasn't prepared to give.

Cassie had success on her second try. Jenny Todd, a fourteen-year-old who lived a mere half a mile down the road and who had filled in before, would be more than glad to stay with Merrie while her mother went for a drive. She said she had exams to study for, and that it would do her good to get away from her noisy younger brother. She could even ride her bike over and back, she said, and would be there in a half hour.

Cassie hung up the phone, eyeing it with mixed emotions. She had no excuse anymore—it was time to face the music. With trembling hands she smoothed the curtain of sun-streaked hair back from her haunted-looking face. The sooner it was done, the sooner the interminable uncertainty would be over. In the last four weeks she had almost hoped Bran would sue her for custody—anything rather than the dreadful limbo in which she'd existed. At least by the time tonight was over, she'd know where she and Merrie stood.

A half hour later she slid onto the wide bench seat of a brand-new luxury American station wagon, which had obviously replaced the battered Mercedes rental. The tension reached out hungry hands toward her, knotting her stomach as he put the car into gear. With shaking fingers she fastened her seat belt, and not a moment too soon. He took off into the night, driving like a demon, taking the corners far too quickly, and keeping the gas pedal to the floor with relentless intensity.

They drove in tense, angry silence for more than twenty minutes, until slowly she felt some of the tension drain from his taut beautiful body, and the pressure on the accelerator let up slightly. With the lessening in speed he opened the window, letting in the damp sea breeze to ruffle his black curls and tease her tendrils of chestnut hair into her face. The warm wet breeze mingled with the faint, always enticing smell of his after-shave, and suddenly an unbidden memory came to Cassie. She had been eight months pregnant, her body large and ungainly as she waddled through the stores, trying to complete her meager Christmas shopping. She ended up in the most expensive department store Bern had to offer, the one that contained the largest selection of men's colognes. She was intent on finding an innocuous present for David Tremayne, her recently acquired boss and friend.

Before she had come within ten feet of the counter, however, her traitorous senses had picked out the enticing aroma of Bran's special after-shave. She'd stood there, blocking the harassed customers in the midst of their last-minute Christmas shopping, and burst into tears.

She wished she could do the same thing right now. The tension and anxiety of the last few weeks had built to exploding level, and as Bran's anger seemed to leave him the strain increased, until she was afraid she might scream.

Finally, she broke the silence, certain she would lose control completely if it continued. "Is this a rented car?" she inquired with an attempt at lightness. "A station wagon hardly seems your type. I'm surprised they let you have another after what happened to the Mercedes."

He cast a small curious glance at her averted profile. "It's mine. I bought it just before I left Virginia."

"You don't have the Jaguar anymore?"

"Oh, I still have it. I decided I needed a larger car if I'm going to have a family."

Her heart began pounding, fast heavy beats that shook her slender frame. "You're that certain you and Lucy will get custody?" she asked calmly enough, her palms wet.

His eyebrows drew together in a sudden scowl. "I thought I told you Lucy and I weren't engaged, had never been, officially. There's only been one woman I've proposed to. I may have a great many faults, but dishonesty isn't one of them."

She had to grant him that, flinching. "Then where do you intend to get your family from?" Her voice was low.

He hesitated for a moment, and Cassie had the absurd notion that he might be uncertain what to say next. But that was impossible. Bran was always in control, always so sure of himself. His next words, however, made her begin to doubt she knew anything at all about him.

He cleared his throat. "I've made arrangements for us to get married in Virginia in three weeks time. We can have the blood work done before we head east, and then there shouldn't be too much delay. I thought the wedding would be small—just Meredith and Gary and Mrs. Bellingson. And your sister, if she wants to come."

"What?"

He ignored her startled cry. "We can live at the farmhouse. Meredith is working for a small nutritional research center over in Bennington. I'm sure you'd have no difficulty in finding a job there if you want to continue working. There's more than enough room for a nursery, and—"

"No." The word came out shaky but definite.

"No?" he echoed, apparently unmoved as he continued to drive, sedately enough now, through the twilight. "Well, I suppose I can always move to Oregon. I like this part of the world—there's something about the wildness and loneliness that calls to me. Do you suppose we could buy your house? Or should we plan to build our own? I'd have to leave the Foundation, but I've always wanted to practice law on my own. I expect I could manage well enough out here, if this is where you want to live."

"No, I won't marry you," she clarified, her voice shaking uncontrollably. "I can't imagine why you would want me to. You'll be able to get partial custody of Merrie—all you have to do is try. I won't fight you on that. You could marry Lucy and set up a nice little family and live happily ever after; you don't have to tie yourself to me."

They were driving along a darkened back road by this time, the gravel surface having little effect on the smooth ride of the big American car. "I don't want to marry Lucy," he replied reasonably enough. "I've never wanted to marry her. I don't know why you keep bringing her up. She was someone to be with when I was lonely, missing you, and that's all. I used her, and she used me—a mutually satisfying relationship, such as it was—but it's over now."

"You don't have to marry me for Merrie's sake," Cassie said wearily, "We can work something out—she won't suffer for it."

Bran's expletive was short and frustrated, and the look he threw her was blazing. "Listen, you little idiot, and stop jumping ahead. I happen to love my daughter and want her to be with me. But that's not enough. I'm greedy, I want it all. And all includes you, too."

It was finally more than Cassie could bear. The sobs that welled up threatened to strangle her, and she finally released them, bursting into uncontrollable weeping as she buried her face in her hands.

A moment later he pulled over to the side of the road, turned off the car, and eased her sobbing figure into his arms.

"Don't cry, Cassie," he murmured brokenly in her ear. "Please, don't cry. I'll do anything you want, anything that will make you happy. But please, I don't think I can bear to lose you again." Desperate hands smoothed her hair away from her tear-streaked face. Panicked kisses covered her cheeks. "I knew where you were for months, but I was afraid to come and find you. I felt so damn guilty about the way I'd treated you, I was afraid you wouldn't have anything to do with me. I tried to redeem myself by clearing your name, but I was afraid that wasn't enough.

"I wanted to kill David Tremayne when he looked at you. I'm a rotten, jealous, lousy kind of guy, Cassie, but I'll try to control it, if only you'll let me try. Please, Cassie, say you'll let me try."

Cassie listened to him in stunned disbelief. Her tears vanished, her trembling increased as his mouth scattered hungry little kisses on her face. She looked up, doubting, tear-filled eyes meeting his desperate ones.

"You still love me?" she whispered, astonished. "How could you possibly after I kept Merrie from you?"

A small hopeful, reluctant smile pulled at one corner of his mouth. "It's hard, believe me," he said softly, the teasing expression in his eyes taking the sting out of his words. "But I realized that I frightened you. And you would have told me sooner or later. Wouldn't you have?" There was still a note of pleading in his strong voice.

"Of course I would have. I hated keeping it from you. But I had to protect Merrie. I was afraid you'd try to take her away from me."

"I want to share her with you. And I want to share you with her. I want us to be a family, Cassie. I should have trusted you, from the very beginning. And you did try to tell me, once she was born."

She pulled away a little from the comforting haven of his arms, and he let her go, reluctantly. "I think the time has come for me to be completely honest," she said in a low voice. "I did think you had a right to know about Merrie. But the main reason I tried to call you was that I was desperate to see you again."

"Why?" His voice was low and intense, as if the world hung on her answer.

"Because I love you, of course," she said softly, giving up her last defense, giving it up gladly as she went back into his arms.

His mouth came down on hers with such overwhelming passion that her senses swam. His lips were fierce and demanding on hers, his tongue tasting the treasures that lurked behind her small white teeth. With a wondrous sense of coming home she gave herself up to the full glory of his embrace, her tongue meeting his with bold desire, until they emerged, breathless.

"God, do you have any idea how long I've waited to hear you say that?" he demanded huskily, cupping her face in his hands. "How many times have I told you that I loved you, waiting for your response?" His mouth began a slow impassioned descent along the sensitive side of her neck.

"But I didn't dare tell you," she murmured against the black silk of his hair. "I was afraid to trust you."

"And do you trust me now, Cassie?" he whispered, his breath warm on her flushed skin above the light cotton sundress. "Tell me you trust me. I need to hear it."

"I trust you, Bran. Completely. With my life. With our daughter's life. I trust you."

His mouth caught hers once more with burning gratitude, as his hands reached up to catch the firm globes of her unbound breasts. He pulled away for a moment, his voice thick with desire. "Are you wearing anything underneath that dress?" he demanded.

"Nothing at all." She smiled up at him helplessly. "I didn't expect you."

"Oh, I wouldn't say that. I think you're perfectly attired for me," he groaned in her ear, his fingers dispensing with the three small buttons that held the loose folds closed about her. After pushing the filmy cotton down to her waist, he bent his head until his mouth caught one taut nipple, already fully aroused by his clever hands.

With a low moan she arched toward him. "Bran, don't do that," she whispered. "I don't think I could bear it if—if—"

"If I stopped?" he finished for her, taking one hand that had been clenched on his shoulder and slipping it inside his shirt, down the warm hair-roughened flesh. "We don't have to stop, Cassie," he murmured against her neck. "And I, for one, sure as hell don't want to. We're on a back road—no one is going to drive by, and if they do, I doubt they'll notice anything. And I don't give a damn if they do. I've waited too long for you. I can't wait any longer—don't ask me to."

The hand that he had placed against his chest slid downward, resting lightly on his belt buckle. "I don't want to wait any longer, either," she whispered, unbuckling his belt with shaking hands,

It took them only a few minutes more of laughter, tears, and fumbling hands to strip away the rest of their clothes. And then he was pushing her gently back against the seat, her hair spread out behind her, as his hands found and readied her. And when she thought she could bear no more, he filled her, making her complete for the first time in her life, complete, fulfilled, and loved. The slow steady rhythm of his lovemaking gnawed at her, eroded away her control, until suddenly her entire body went rigid, and her voice cried out, "Bran, don't...leave me," as wave after wave of pulsating ecstasy washed over her.

"I won't," he whispered in her ear, his hands cupping her buttocks to pull her closer against him. "I never will." And then he followed her, and the sound of her name on his lips was sweet in her ear.

What seemed like hours later she heard a soft disconcerting chuckle in her ear. "I hate to have to do this, Cassie," he whispered, "but I'm afraid I'm going to have to sit up. The steering wheel is digging into my back, and my legs are in the strangest position."

She smiled up at him, blissfully sated, and reached up to lightly brush her lips against his before releasing him with great reluctance. "I would have thought you'd be adept at making love in the front seat of a car," she teased.

"I haven't tried it since I was a teenager," he said, sliding behind the steering wheel in a sitting position, magnificently, unconsciously male in his nudity. He slanted a wicked smile in her direction. "It wasn't as much fun back then."

"The practice is good for you," she teased, pulling herself reluctantly into a sitting position and reaching for the sundress that lay on the floor of the car. "I'm feeling quite insatiable at the thought of being married to you. I like the idea of making love to you in a car. We should try the Jaguar when we get back to Virginia."

He groaned in mock dismay. "We'll never manage."

"Of course we will!" she shot back. "I have complete faith in your ingenuity." When the dress was buttoned around her, she slid over and curled up against him, his arm drawing her closer against the warmth of his bare shoulder.

"Are you sure you want to live in Virginia?" he queried." "We don't have to...."

"I'd love it. But it would be nice if we could visit here every now and then," she said somewhat wistfully.

"We can do better than that. We'll buy your house and keep it for vacations, whenever we need to get away. How does that sound?"

"Heavenly," she murmured, letting her lips graze one of his flat masculine nipples. Her mischievous eyes could see quite clearly his reaction in the darkened car, and she doubled her efforts.

"Cassie, Cassie," he groaned.

She laughed. "I told you I was insatiable."

"In which case, I think we'd better see about some sort of protection. Unless you've already done something about it?" There was slight diffidence in his voice, which Cassie intended to banish once and for all.

"Nope. I've lived a celibate life away from you, Bran Rathburne. And knowing how fertile we are, I would guess that we might already be too late."

He was very still, his heart beating loudly in her ear. "Would you mind very much?"

She smiled up at him. "Not a bit. I figure I owe you nine months of pregnancy. And you owe me a hand to hold during delivery. Is it a deal?"

His mouth came down on hers, lightly, reverently, sealing an unspoken vow. "A deal," he agreed softly.

While leaning back against the leather seat Cassie

watched him with half-closed eyes as he pulled his jeans back on and started the car. Never had she felt so at peace, so buoyant. "By the way, Bran," she said softly, her lips teasing the line of his shoulder.

"Hmmm?"

"Merrie sleeps through the night."

Bran's eyes met hers, smiling down with an expression that promised more than any human had a right to expect. "Good" was all he said. And pulling her willing body closer against him, he started down the road.